GIRL SCOUTS AND CADET GROUPS WITH TRINITARIAN SISTER

Joan standing next to Sister Mary Genevieve -

THE FIREFLIES OF WECCACOE

Joan Morrisroe Reynolds

authorHOUSE®

AuthorHouse™
1663 Liberty Drive, Suite 200
Bloomington, IN 47403
www.authorhouse.com
Phone: 1-800-839-8640

First published by AuthorHouse 8/14/2008

ISBN: 978-1-4343-6829-4 (sc)

Library of Congress Control Number: 2008901960

Printed in the United States of America
Bloomington, Indiana

This book is printed on acid-free paper.

This book is dedicated to the memory of my beloved son,

Francis Patrick Malloy
7/20/1956-6/14/2004

Bright Be the Place of thy Soul

"No lovelier spirit than thine
E'er burst from its mortal control,
In the orbs of the blessed to shine.
On earth thou wert all but divine,
As thy soul shall immortally be;
And our sorrow may cease to repine,
When we know that thy God is with thee."

Lord Byron

ACKNOWLEDGEMENTS

My husband, Bob Reynolds. He has supported every endeavor that I have undertaken. He is the wind beneath my ability to soar.

My son, M. Shawn Malloy, one of the most gifted people that I have ever encountered. Shawn is a hero in his own right.

My daughter, Mary-Malloy Bucher, who has spent countless hours researching with me.

Frank Mungiovi, a true friend, a published author and technical computer consultant throughout my writing this book.

Angelo Monlinari, for the illustrations, including the front cover.

Melissa McFarland, an expert on technical issues. She helped me work out many of the glitches I had encountered.

THE Fireflies OF Weccacoe
Joan Morrisroe Reynolds
THE Fireflies OF Weccacoe
Reynolds

Some names have been changed to protect the guilty

<Lenape Indian Words> followed by their meanings

FORWARD

This story takes place in South Philly, in historic Philadelphia, Pennsylvania. It describes the World War II era through the eyes of a child. The terror-stricken child hid behind the living room sofa after she heard the news that the Japanese had bombed Pearl Harbor, Hawaii on December 7, 1941. She was afraid to go to the breakfast room because it had a skylight and she thought the bombs would come through it. She forgot her Christmas pageant that was scheduled for that afternoon.

The story revolves around a precocious child who has a flair to make money through operating her own businesses. She believes she has the genes of David Rittenhouse, her ancestor and the first director of the United States Mint.

She describes discovering Weccacoe in the 1940s. It was a fun place to go. She picked wildflowers and caught lightening bugs. Eventually it becomes a special place. She realizes that Weccacoe reinforces that there is a connection between the human spirit and the spirit of the universe. She describes tragic events eloquently.

She introduces readers to the Mummers, a pivotal part of a Philadelphia tradition. Many historic sites are mentioned with narratives about them as well.

She describes events going on in her own little world as well as the world at large. She describes attending Sacred Heart School and Sacred Heart of Jesus Church. She describes being exposed to all of the cultural arts in that little parish on the waterfront district of South Philly.

CHAPTER 1

My memories of growing up in South Philadelphia are treasures that I have stored in the tabernacle of my mind. Over the years, I have had people approach me to inquire about interesting, long forgotten events that had occurred in our neighborhood on the waterfront district during the World War II era. My book will shed light on these events. There are some other times immortalized as well. Most are events in history, such as the snowfall of 1888, which was related to me by my Grampy Brennan. Although we have had heavier snowfalls, the snowfall of 1888 had paralyzed the entire East Coast of the country. He said that most of the New England cities and states had been more harshly hit than Philadelphia. He went on to say that, Cape Cod and Rhode Island had escaped some of Mother Nature's wrath. People in those New England areas had some mobility; streets were shoveled out and sleds could be used as emergency vehicles. When he related the story of the blizzard of 1888, intellectually it seemed like the Stone Age to me. However, how he related the story enabled me to feel as though I was there in that quaint little house in Queen's Village on that snowy day so long ago. He described waking up early on that Monday morning, March 12, 1888, to the sight of snow up to his bedroom window that was on the second story of his home. He uttered <hoh> an exclamation of surprise. The rooftops were covered with mounds of snow; and the feathers of snow continued to flurry from the sky. Flickers of color played an elusive game of hide and seek; like slippery little elves trying to elude detection. He thought of gemstones when he saw the glittering colors of silver, blue and the occasional red. He described the sound of silence that the snowfall had induced. He knew he would not be hearing the clop, clop, clop of the horses' hooves against the cobblestones that lined Federal Street. The sight of the falling feathery snowflakes reminded him of his eiderdown comforter that brought him the warmth and comfort that he needed on that snowy day in 1888. He told me that it made him feel so safe, so cozy and so at one with the universe. In addition, there was no school! People could think things out for themselves without the modern conveniences of electricity, radios and televisions. The smells of bacon and eggs permeated the house. The bread was toasted by frying it a light coating of the bacon grease. He was summoned to eat breakfast at eight a.m. The entire family sat down together for the special occasion of the blizzard of 1888. The family together and the delicious breakfast more than compensated for not having milk delivered that morning. Mother Nature provided the ice for the perishables.

The Franklin stove worked furiously to keep the tiny colonial style home warm. When he told me about the Franklin stove, I visualized the flames dancing a flamenco to the packed audience of the snow. It was a standing room only type of audience peeping through the windows. Oil lamps lit the individual rooms.

We decided to renovate a house on Porter Street in South Philly. It was in the same waterfront district where I had spent my childhood. We bought it in July 2003. Our son, Michael Shawn Malloy, whom we call Shawn, rewired the house. In the middle bedroom, we discovered a small bump protruding out of the long wall that faced the entry door to the room. I began to recall Grampy Brennan's story of the oil lamps that lit each room of his colonial style home during the snowstorm of 1888. Although the move had been planned for a few years, when the time came to sell our house on Academy Road and move, I found it difficult. My husband, Bob, viewed the move as a place where he would not have to mow lawns, varnish decks or pay the high taxes of Northeast Philadelphia. I looked at it in a nostalgic way. I remembered Bob and my wedding day. He looked so handsome. I visualized seeing our three children coming through the door with baseball mitts, bats and gloves. I recalled Mary's bridal day. She was so beautiful. She had nine bridesmaids. An old time trolley car sat outside our house to take them to the church. The house had been decorated with flowers and bells and a lit arched arbor decorated the front door. She was married at five p.m. on the evening after Thanksgiving in 1986. I saw all of Mary's dolls throughout the years. Some even adorned the bed in her room long after Mary had moved into her own home. I thought of how the house had served us so well during the years. It was a happy home. We had so much fun in it. My mother spent some time with us during her final days. I remember her saying, "You really enjoy your home and you encourage others to enjoy it as well." That is about how it was. Bob was her caregiver for the short time that she stayed with us. I was still working.

Bob had recently retired from his second career. He had served as a Philadelphia Police Detective. Before retiring from the Police Department, he attended LaSalle University. He earned a degree in Psychology in three years. I recalled the party that the family had hosted for him. Oh, there were so many good memories. I was not ready to sell our home yet, no, not yet. Then there were the fun times I had with our youngins as I playfully called them. I have had so many adventures or misadventures with them, depending on how one looks at them. One stood out that day. I do not know why it stood out at that particular time. It was not Christmastime. Bob and I had taken four of our grandchildren to see the movie, The Nutcracker, in Feasterville, Bucks County, Pennsylvania. They sat mesmerized for a very short time. They sat still for about ten minutes, then one climbed over the seat, one lost a shoe, one filled their diaper with a super duper, a real stinker. We then realized that we had the entire left rows of the theater all to ourselves. When we arrived home, everybody was washed. The baby was given a bath and a change of diaper. As I was carrying the concealed contents of the baby diaper to the trash that was to be picked up the next morning, a gentleman passing our house offered to take the bag and place it atop the trash pile. He carried the bag of shit to the curb for me. Chivalry is not dead. I stopped and talked with Sally Connors, our neighbor of many years. Our neighbors were like family. I then went back into the house. Once again, everyone washed his or her hands and we sat down to tea. Our two-year-old grandson was having so much fun with us that he decided to join the four females at the tea party. Bob declined. He told us that he would be right back. I think he went to purchase some aspirin. We needed another cup since our grandson was joining us at the tea party. I picked up a miniature cup that Mary had used as a child. It had a gold rim. It had a beautiful white dove that was flying into the heavens. It was flying up into the snowflakes that were flurrying from the skies. The background color on the cup was light blue. I looked at it and observed that it was a peaceful, beautiful scene.

Everyone reassured me that we would still have these priceless memories. Logically, I knew this. I also knew that we would be creating new precious memories in our new home. However, something was gnawing at me from inside. I did not think we would ever be able to find neighbors as good as our neighbors. We watched out for each other. We never had to worry about going on trips. If anyone tried to break into our house, they would have the Connors, the Woehlkes, The Naughtons, and anyone else who happened to be around chasing them. That is how it was; better neighbors could not be found anywhere. I visualized Franny and Shawn tossing the football back and forth with Dave Warren, Butch Benedict, Charlie Meyer and Brian Austin. Carlos and Bobby Villaneuva were always in our house. I thought of the Garritys. They were getting ready to make a move also, in order to downsize. Where did the years go? I was young with young children when I bought the house in the new development called Engelwood, which is in the Far Northeast section of Philadelphia. On summer evenings, the large backyard sounded like a jungle. One year the cicadas were out making their particular chirr sounds. There were the swimming pools and the laughter of children. The smells of the barbeques cooking dinner were mouth watering. I knew that we would be asked to join someone for a hamburger or steak or just a taste of a newly concocted salad made by someone from his or her vivid imagination. The green, green grass of the large back yard was always neatly manicured. We had a big oak tree in the back yard. We watched it grow. It was now reaching up into the heavens. In 1980, I had picked a one-inch potential Blue Spruce tree. It sprang up rapidly. Amazingly, it was just a twig when I picked it. I called it the Franny Viera tree in memory of my friend Franny who passed away at a far too early age. She had been hosting us at her home in the Pocono Mountains of Pennsylvania. I picked that twig from the woods across from her Chalet type home. I planted it before she died. After she died, I thought of her every time I looked at it. We decided to postpone moving into our new home. We rented out the newly renovated home until I was sure the time was right to make the move.

On June 14, 2004, I was having lunch with a few of my friends. The misgivings became more powerful than ever. It was not about the houses or anything material. It was much more than that. I did not know what but I do know that I never had a premonition like that before in my entire life. It was as if my soul was screaming out. I hurriedly excused myself and left the luncheon. My friends were puzzled. Maureen ran after me to inquire what was wrong. I responded that I did not know. She asked me if I wanted her to go with me. I thanked her but replied, "No." I was in a tizzy. It was so out of character for me. After I left the luncheon, I hurried home. As I was changing into clothing that was more casual on that humid day in June, a knock came on the door. The bell rang. The knocking continued onto the window. Initially, I thought that someone had forgotten his or her key. I then realized that it was more than that. It was definitely more than that. I did not want to go downstairs and open the door to destiny. I knew, I just knew. It was innate. I opened the door. I recognized Les Yost immediately. He was president of the Philadelphia, Pennsylvania Firefighters' Union. He looked at me and asked if someone was sick; he went on to say that, they received a call that someone was sick. He was gentle and tried to smooth the way for me. I uttered, "Oh, something must have happened to Bob and Franny must have taken him to the hospital." I dreaded what was happening on that Monday afternoon around two p.m. Les called around in order to locate which hospital the "sick" person had been taken. I then called my grandson Stephen. I asked Stephen if he knew what was going on. He replied in a monotone almost robotic tone. "Grandmom, Uncle Franny had a heart attack, he died." It sounded as though he wanted me to reassure him that it was all a bad dream. He was in shock. I was paralyzed. I thought that it could not be so; it just could not be true. Les drove me to Saint Mary's Hospital in Langhorne, Pennsylvania. I held onto the rosary beads that my friend Maureen had brought me back from her trip to Ireland. I fingered the beads but that is all I could do. When we arrived at Saint Mary's Hospital, I saw Franny. He already had been pronounced dead. I was screaming, "Franny wake up, please wake up." However he did not wake up, he was gone. His face was angelic looking. He had two marks on the left side of his forehead from where he had fallen. He had been given the last rites of the Catholic Church. When I saw the look on his face, I knew that he was with God.

In February 2004, I had received a telephone call from my son Shawn. He told me that Franny had suffered a heart attack after fighting a fire. I remember the paralyzed feeling that came over me. Shawn told me not to worry as Franny was going to be okay. Franny was released from the hospital the next morning and told to see his personal physician. He called me at our winter home in Fort Myers, Florida. I told him that he better not have had a heart attack after all the good healthy foods that I had fed him when he was growing up. We had the gift of laughter in our family. He told me to put my mind at ease that it was not my cooking that caused him to pass out on the job. I think that maybe all the smoke and fire may have contributed to it, he added. Never did it enter my mind or anyone else's mind in the family that it was an undetected heart attack. His personal physician advised him to retire. He knew Franny suffered from his back because of carrying people from burning buildings. He knew all the gallantry that Franny's job had encompassed. The most recent was his carrying a mother and a small baby to safety. Oh, he was a hero; we have the certificates of valor and heroism to prove it. For me, there was always a veil there. I never wanted to look behind it. I did not want to think of my son working such a hazardous job. There were stories and pictures of him in the local newspapers from time to time. They were about his heroism and valor. There was also a story about his capability to diagnose and repair any problem with equipment that was used at the firehouse. There was a picture of his handsome, smiling face. Firefighters refer to their station as their house and they bond like family. When people work side by side like that and do not know if all will be present to answer the next roll call, the silent covenant is strong. Shortly after Franny died, two firefighters were killed. One firefighter, Rey Rubio was trapped. His captain, John Taylor would not leave him; they both died. The cause of the fire was that a man had been growing marijuana inside a house in the Kensington section of Philadelphia, Pennsylvania. When I think of Franny and all of the other firefighters who have paid the ultimate sacrifice, I recall the words of Jesus, "Greater love than this hath no man than to lay down his life for another." I have so many people around me who truly love me; I would not have been able to go on breathing without them. I know that every firefighter is a daily hero, sometimes simply by showing up for work, especially after there had been a horrific fire or a catastrophe.

I remember the Gulf Oil Refinery. On August 17, 1975, eight firefighters had lost their lives battling the inferno at The Gulf Oil Refinery in South Philadelphia. They were sons, husbands, fathers and brothers, doing their job that day. Shortly before six a.m. on that infamous day, a seventy-five thousand tank at the refinery was being filled with crude oil mixed with naphtha from a tanker ship. Vapors from the tank seeped into the boiler house causing an explosion that reminded me of Hiroshima; that occurred on August 6, 1945. The Enola Gay, the American B-29, Super Fortress airplane dropped a bomb over Hiroshima, Japan. Nagasaki was then targeted. On August 9, 1945, the American B-29 airplane, The Bockscar, dropped an atomic bomb on Nagasaki. That led to the ending of World War II. The Japanese had started World War II with America with a sneak attack at the United States Naval Station at Pearl Harbor, Hawaii. Their bombs have entombed thousands of American sailors. The fire at the Gulf Oil Refinery was considered under control and manageable by eight a.m. Around four forty p.m. fire flashed from beneath an apparatus used to spread foam on the petroleum products. It spread rapidly across the 732-acre complex. The cloud of smoke and the smells of oil, naphtha, and the unthinkable loss of lives permeated the Philadelphia area. On August 15, 2007, there was a ceremony at the Fireman's Hall Museum on Second Street near Race Street in Olde City, Philadelphia. They were officially honored with plaques on August 15, 2007. Philadelphia Fire Commissioner Lloyd

Ayers read the names of those claimed by the August 17, 1975 blaze at the Gulf Oil Refinery. Over 200 people attended. Many were the survivors of the fallen heroes. How did they go on breathing after such an unfathomable loss? I believe that the human spirit is part of the Divine Spirit. I believe what the Native American Indians believe. They call it <Manitto> Great White Spirit. I believe what I was taught at Sacred Heart School. Our bodies are tabernacles of the Holy Spirit.

I remembered the prayer that I had been saying when the firefighters were battling the blaze at the Gulf Oil Refinery in 1975. The nuns taught me to recite the Hail Mary often and especially if the death of someone was near. I said the Hail Mary then and again on August 15, 2007. When I recite the Hail Mary, I feel as though they are not alone when they leave this plane of existence.

The Hail Mary:

Hail Mary full of grace
The Lord is with thee
Blessed art thou among women
And blessed is the fruit of thy womb, Jesus,

Holy Mary, mother of God
Pray for us sinners,
Now and at the hour of our death.
Amen.

For whom the bells tolled:

Firefighter	John J. Anderson	🔔
Firefighter	Hugh J. McIntyre	🔔
Firefighter	Ralph J. Campana	🔔
Firefighter	Joseph R. Wiley	🔔
Firefighter	Rodger T. Parker	🔔
Firefighter	Robert J. Fisher	🔔
Firefighter	Carroll K. Brenek	🔔
Lieutenant	James J. Pouliot	🔔

I do not think that any firefighter who paid the ultimate price of laying down their life trying to save another or fighting a fatal fire realized that they were kissing their loved ones for the last time. I do not think they realized that risk when they were describing to a child what they would do together when the firefighter was off from work.

Many times, I have witnessed firefighters doing their jobs. Sometimes it was putting out a fire. At other times, it could be any type of emergency imaginable. The critical tasks that the firefighters perform every day take a toll on each one of them. Some are better at disguising it than others. Franny needed to leave many family celebrations early because of his jobs. He always held another job besides his job as a firefighter as many firefighters do. He whispered to me at his daughter Jessica's graduation from Saint Basils Academy, "It's all worth it." He then proudly presented her with the most beautiful bouquet of red roses that I have ever seen.

After Franny died, I walked around in a fog for six months. I had lost so much weight that people were beginning to be concerned. Someone casually remarked that I was too skinny. I thanked them for their concern and then told them that I believe one can never be too thin or too rich. Something was happening for me. I was beginning to regain some of my sense of humor. I also knew that if I did not start writing, I would never be able to recover from the loss of my son. I thought that I would write about him. It tended to open the hole in my heart even wider. I received divine inspiration to write about my colorful childhood.

No way did I ever dream that I would be writing a book about the South Philly waterfront district when we bought the house on Porter Street in 2003. I tearfully said goodbye to our neighbors in Englewood, which everyone calls Parkwood. Two different builders built Parkwood and Englewood. Over the years, Englewood just evolved into Parkwood. The houses are intermingled.

We bought the house on Porter Street from Joe Pooler and his sister, Margaret Pooler Dunn. Margaret's house is next door to ours. I enjoy spending time on the front porch with her. There is no separation between the porches. There is no fence between our yards. We like it that way. Shawn and I were in the middle bedroom. He was going to build a large walk in closet. The house was built around the turn of the twentieth century. There was no need for large closets then. There was a doorway between the master bedroom and the middle bedroom. I recalled the closets in our house on Front Street in the 1940s. We had a Sunday coat and a weekday coat. The accessories such as gloves and hats went on a shelf on top of the little closet inside the doorway to the cellar. Our boots for rainy and snowy days were taken off in the vestibule of our house. In the summer, they were stored in a hanging wooden storage bin in the cellar. My father had constructed it. Two long slats suspended it from the ceiling. He had them suspended so we could reach the bin. However, times have changed. Another door and wall were to be put in the middle bedroom. I was looking at the bump on the wall, the remnants of the oil lamp. We decided to keep it. I thought of Grampy Brennan. Shawn was by the newly installed colonial style window. He said, "Look mama, it's snowing." I took a quantum leap from March 1888 to December 2004. We stood there silently. As I looked at the snowflakes falling, I thought of a poem entitled, The First Snowfall by Russell Lowell Emerson. I am a lover of poetry. I remembered all of the stanzas. As we stood there in silence, I recalled how eloquently the poet had reflected on the first snowfall that had occurred after the death of his daughter. It touched my heart personally on that particular day. He described the power of the snow to mask the scars of his broken heart. He described the mound of snow providing a cover for his little loved one. As if Shawn and I were in harmony, he leaned over and kissed me. I in turn kissed him back two times.

REST IN PEACE MY BELOVED SON FRANNY.

Firefighter Fran Malloy
Germantown Avenue and Somerset Street, Philadelphia, Pa.
Ladder 12-12/08/1990

Philadelphia Fire Department

Merit

On February 4, 1994, at 4503 N. Reese Street,

Firefighter Francis Malloy

of Ladder Company 12, Platoon D, did, without regard for his own personal safety, rescue a civilian from his two story burning dwelling.

Arriving companies encountered heavy fire on the second floor of a two story occupied dwelling. Members were notified of a trapped civilian on the second floor. As members initiated ventilation operations with 1 3/4" waterline, portable ladders were raised for search and rescue. Despite intense heat and dense smoke conditions, FF McNally, along with another firefighter, located the unconscious victim on the second floor rear. Together they removed the unconscious victim to Medic Unit personnel who began advanced life support services.

These courageous actions, under very dangerous conditions, are in keeping with the high traditions of the Philadelphia Fire Department.

Edward G Rendell

MAYOR

June 24, 1995

DATE

FIRE COMMISSIONER

13

CHAPTER 2

Handel's arioso, The Messiah, jarred me out of the hypnotic state. It was the seasonal sound on Shawn's cell phone. The person on the other end of the phone was calling to give Shawn his work schedule for the following week. Downstairs, the front door opened. Bob was coming into the house from his daily walk. My daughter, Mary and my granddaughters, Molly and Audrey followed him into the house. I was going shopping with Mary, Molly and Audrey. We were going to Delaware and Oregon Avenues. Delaware Avenue's name has been changed to Columbus Boulevard. Most neighborhood people still call it Delaware Avenue; after all, that is where it all began, at Delaware Avenue and Shackamaxon Street. History books indicate that the beach like setting with the Lenape Native American Indians and the settlers was at that location. William Penn stood among them. The first Native American was holding onto a one-foot long peace pipe that bellowed gray smoke into the atmosphere. The settlers were bearing gifts of cloth, modern tools and pots that would serve to make life easier for the Native Americans. Prior to the settlers bringing gifts, the Lenape Native Americans clothing was made from animal furs or skins depending on what season it was at the time. The clothing was sewn together with wild grass or anything that would serve to hold it together. The settlers brought them sewing equipment. Everybody seemed happy. I never knew the Penn Treaty Park as it is depicted in history books. The National Sugar Refinery stood at Delaware Avenue and Shackamaxon Street. Penn Treaty Park as I knew it was a stone's throw away. It went unattended for decades. It was surrounded by industry. Philadelphia had grown into the largest, most prosperous city in the English Colonies. Street names have been changed. That is a constant in Philadelphia. I heard a story about a police officer who discovered a dead horse at Delaware Avenue and Shackamaxon Street. His lieutenant picked up the phone and asked if the police officer could kindly drag the horse to Girard Avenue, so they could spell it.

I do recall one incident at Penn Treaty Park during World War II. The police came and burned the weed-strewn lot. I heard the word marijuana. When I went to bed that night, I had some time to think. I derived a conclusion. Those Indians sure did look happy. I thought it was the sight of the gifts from the settlers. They brought food and recipes. The aroma of some of the foods permeated the air before the settlers even approached the Native American Indians. However, something puzzled me. It was the mystery of the peace pipe. My Uncle Sam smoked a pipe. His pipe never bellowed gray smoke into the air like the pipe of the Native Americans. Maybe their brains were fried from smoking pot in the peace pipe. Maybe a seed took root and now almost three hundred years later, it grew out of control. <A> indeed. I do know they were upset when they realized that the land was not theirs anymore. They had thought they were just sharing it. Some of them rebelled by going on <allamuins> war whoops. It was not a safe time to go out in the evenings. There also were wolves running around the muck and mire of the unpaved streets. I related my mystery solving skills to Aunt Mary. She said, "Never." She went on to inform me that William Penn would not go for such nonsense. She said William Penn was a Quaker. He believed Divinity was right inside each one of us. The Lenape Native Americans believed in the <Manitto> Great White Spirit. I said that it was just a thought. Then I retracted my deduction. I did not think they would want to kill the Divinity right inside each one of them. I rethought it and concluded that is what they were doing when they drank the firewater. The Native Americans named the liquor firewater. I did not say anymore; I just thought. In the late 1600s, liquor was banned for the Native Americans because of the war whoops. That made life safer for the bounty hunters to capture the wolves. There was a bounty for bringing in the head of a wolf.

The wolves were considered less dangerous than the <tomahawks> hatchets.

The British drove most of the Lenape Indians out of their homeland. They are not extinct as many writings indicate. Some joined other tribes; some went to Oklahoma. Some went to Canada. Some stayed right there in our neighborhood of Southwark. Southwark and Wiccacoe are intermingled in some areas of South Philadelphia. The Native Americans who remained in the neighborhood intermarried. The only way one could tell if they were descendants of the Lenape Indians is if they would tell you.

Ellie Kiwiken patched up all the bruises and lacerations that the kids in the neighborhood received. She was Native American descent. It was evident. Her skin was golden tan and she wore her long jet-black hair tied back with a big plait extending from the back of her head to her waist. Ellie's teenage daughter, Lily, sang opera. She was great; however, when she belted out those high notes, I thought for sure the rest of the tribe was hiding somewhere, getting ready to bring back the <allamuins>. Galena Waters showed us how to make beaded jewelry. She was a big woman with red hair. She was very gentle. She was much lighter than Ellie; however, her heritage was evident. She was gifted with the natural ability of growing plants and vegetable seeds in a little garden in the back of her house. She knew exactly what to do in order to have them bloom into the largest flowers and vegetables possible. Not only the soil, water and sun produced them. She talked to them and they listened. I do not know what she said. I could not understand the language that she used. I remember one word, <saken>. I know now that it is a Lenape Indian word, meaning shoot forth, spring up.

There was one Indian man who stood outside of the Mom and Pop store at Front and Mountain Streets. He appeared in the early evening and just stood there for hours. He never bothered anyone and no one ever bothered him. He was a short elderly man. We just thought that he wanted to be a wooden Indian that often adorned the entrance of a store. If he was planted there to spy during World War II, he was definitely out of luck. In our neighborhood, we believed loose lips could send someone to jail. The saying was nothing new to us when the government proclaimed, "Loose lips might sink ships."

A love smitten young lady could tip a spy off, simply by saying on which ship her boyfriend was serving.

Mary, Molly, Audrey and I left to go shopping. The snow did not materialize into anything great. The day turned into a Spring like day. While driving east on Oregon Avenue, the aroma emitting from the hot sandwich shop enticed us to stop and eat there. The man took our order. I ordered a cheese steak, Mary and Molly and Audrey ordered a cheese steak. The man yelled to the cook, "four chezes." Mary ordered coffee. The man yelled, "One cawfee." You see, South Philly has a language all its own. The only people who completely understand it are other South Philly people.

We ate outside under the canopy covered with pictures of movie stars, singers and dignitaries who have eaten there and had endorsed it. I ate half of my cheese steak. Something positively was happening for me. Maybe I was starting to heal. A group of people sitting at the table next to ours started to sing Christmas carols. Someone was singing, "We'll bring you some piggy pudding and a cup of good cheer." We laughed and when we returned to the car, we started to sing and act silly. We sang, "We wish you a Merry Christmas and a Happy New Year. We'll bring you some figgy pudding topped with a piggy's toe nail." A short distance away from the eatery we passed Weccacoe Avenue. Molly asked me what kind of name was Weccacoe. I explained that it was a Native American Indian name. The name first appeared where Gloria Dei Church was built in 1681. The spelling the Swedes used was Wiccacoe; however, it is just a deviation of the same name. I told them how special Weccacoe was to me when I was growing up in that little South Philly waterfront neighborhood. I told them that we discovered Weccacoe in the 1940s when we went there to pick cattails. We called them punks. They kept the mosquitoes away. The stores sold them for five cents each. We picked them free. Everything was free on Weccacoe. That is all I said about Weccacoe that day. I needed to keep it in my heart for a while. I revisited Weccacoe in a spiritual sense.

When we reached Delaware Avenue, now Columbus Boulevard, I told them that all of our ancestors had arrived in America via the Delaware River. I told them about the Rittenhouse family. They were gifted American patriots. They came to America by schooner.

They originally arrived on the shore of the lower colony of Delaware. They associated with William Penn, George Washington, Thomas Jefferson and all the notables of that era. I told them about David Rittenhouse being the first director of the United States Mint. David was born in America. I always liked that about David, as I always had my eye on the money. It was not on a grand scale like David Rittenhouse. I was the proprietor of a cigar box. It held the money from two of my businesses. I used bingo chips and newspaper cut to the size of dollar bills for my first business. I ran three businesses of my own even before I started Sacred Heart of Jesus School. I definitely had the genes of David Rittenhouse. I encouraged them to look up all his accomplishments on the computer. He had so many accomplishments; I would need to write a tome on David. My grandmother was Ella Rittenhouse. She died at age forty, long before I was born. We never knew any of the Rittenhouse family. My grandmother was a WASP, White Anglo Saxon Protestant, until she converted to Catholicism. I derived a conclusion that there were some things we just never would be told. Airing out one's business was taboo in those days. Maybe that is why people died young.

Of course, I had been warned by Aunt Mary to leave the detective work to the detectives. She always added that I have a good head on my shoulders. She did not want to discourage me from trying to figure things out on my own. I just think she was afraid I would investigate her. However, that was only a thought and I never mentioned it to her or to anyone else. The first thing I would have asked my father's sister, Aunt Mary, was why she married grouchy Uncle Sam Coarse, who everyone called Sam Cross. Uncle Sam never gave me any problems. He did not like my brother, Bobby. Uncle Sam always sat in the dining room. He dressed in a multi-colored silk smoking jacket. It had red dragons, emitting fire from their noses. It had black cuffs. It had speckles of gold, white and green throughout it. He had a smoking area prepared with a pipe rack, pipe cleaners and tobacco pouches. One day he was sitting in the dining room of our house that use to be their house. He sat right under the banister. It was a beautiful piece of architect with a biblical woman holding a high basket over her head. The basket lit up to present a golden glow. I slid down the banister and heard my father yell, "Watch out, it's going to hit the Cuckoo." He did not even get to say clock before it came crashing down on Uncle Sam. I had just turned five years of age a few days before that infamous incident, so I thought he was calling Uncle Sam, The Cuckoo. After that incident, that is what I called him, Uncle Cuckoo. If I needed to lay down the law about his crankiness with Bobby, I would just call him Cuckoo and then he knew I meant business.

Even though Aunt Mary had told me to leave the detective work to the detectives, I still could think things out without mentioning them to anyone. Of course, it would be two more years before I was to reach the age of reason. I allowed myself a margin of error until I reached the age of reason.

In late Spring of 1940, I spilled a pot of boiling French fry grease over my entire left arm. My cousin, Nuny Wootten, ran to get her grandmother, Mrs. Gilbert, who was a faith healer. She was an elegant tall, trim woman. She wore her white hair in a bun on the back of her head. She dressed impeccably. She wore black spats over her white shoes. Spats are cloth or leather shoe coverings. They were popular at the turn of the twentieth century. After that day, we never laughed about her wearing spats again. She stood over me, prayed and made motions around my arm. Of course, she could not touch my arm. Any evidence of a burn disappeared. We were in awe. We believed in miracles; however, we thought only Catholics could accomplish them. Here was Mrs. Gilbert, a WASP, pulling one off. <Lo> see, behold.

My mother asked her what she said in order to get the miracle. She responded that it is a prayer that we say every day. I immediately thought of the Our Father; however, I now know that the gift of healing was hers. I did not know it then when I was only five years of age. When Mrs. Gilbert was leaving; she patted me on the head and said, "Your grandmother was from a good old Methodist family." Then I knew there were things that we did not know; and probably would never be told in this lifetime.

One day shortly after the healing, Aggie Winters and I found a dead sparrow. I told her that I knew how to bring the little bird back to life. I told her to watch me. I said the Our Father over the bird. Nothing happened. Oh, I forgot the motions. I then performed all the motions around the bird while saying the Our Father to myself. I did not share my secret of how to resurrect the bird with Aggie, and then she would be a healer too. The sparrow was still dead. Aggie said, "I knew you couldn't bring that bird back to life." I pondered. I said, "Let's bury it and we'll come back tomorrow and try again. It took Jesus three days to resurrect. My mother told me that." She was skeptical but agreed. We went the next day and dug up the dead bird. It was still dead. We went the next day, the third day, the days of days. Zilch! The sparrow was still dead. After that, we went about once a week. I was not one to give up easily. I chanted and silently said the Our Father and made the motions. Zilch! Then about a month after we found the dead bird, we dug where we had it buried but it was gone. It would have been nice if it had waited until we were there to see it fly up into the heavens. However, it was not there. Word soon spread in our neighborhood. People in our neighborhood usually did not ask questions from point A to point B. If they heard the story, it was gospel. After that, people would come to their front doors and ask me to pray for them. Usually it would be a prayer involving the street number that was to come out that day. Number writing and number playing were big businesses in our neighborhood when I was growing up. I always liked the set up on Mountain Street. The south side of Mountain Street was lined with fences where the yards from the houses on Morris Street stood. I liked the set up because the people who lived on the north side of Morris Street actually had two streets for the price of one. It especially came in handy for the number writers who lived on the north side of Morris Street. They could operate their business from the back of the house, which was on Mountain Street. The gate was open and a person could just walk into the little kitchen where the number writer was sitting at their kitchen table. There were no age requirements to place a bet on a number. It was not a lottery as we have today. It was against the law. There was always a number backer. The number backer drove a big, beautiful car. He traded it in every year for the newest model. Business was good. It was not too shabby for the people in our neighborhood either. Someone hit the numbers everyday. That would give the neighborhood people hope in desperate times. Therefore, when a person in our neighborhood

21

asked me to pray that they would win the illegal lottery based on a winning horse race, I did. I never did anything without thinking out the moral implications of it. I would not pray for a burglar to have a good cache. However, with the state our country was in due to the Great Depression, I thought it would be the lesser of two evils to pray for someone to hit the numbers. When War World II was going on and the fear of who would be getting the next telegram to inform them that their son was missing in action; I knew that it was absolutely the lesser of two evils. It gave the people in our neighborhood hope for the day. It kept their minds occupied. If their number came out, it led them to believe that they were on a lucky streak. Since they were on a lucky streak, they thought their loved ones were being protected over there. There were other number writers who covered various territories in our little waterfront neighborhood. Some walked around and a person simply walked up to them and placed a bet. We liked Joe Riter so much. He would pass our window every day and joke with us. We would joke back and yell, "Dopey Joe, dopey Joe." He would claw his hand and make a motion that he was coming after us. We then laughed and laughed. We looked forward to seeing him come past our house every day. Then there was Rebecca. Rebecca was the essence of a lady. She was a beautiful elderly woman with blue eyes that showed she had a good soul. She wore starched cotton dresses in the 1940s. The dress always had two deep pockets in it. She was about five feet tall. Her hair was always curled and she was just a beautiful person. Any child would be proud to have her for their grandmother.

Grampy Brennan went to the hearings at the police station at Fourth Street and Snyder Avenue every morning. He was retired. He had several friends who attended the hearings with him. He came into our house one day and told us that when the lawbreakers lined up in front of Magistrate Meyers, the Magistrate almost jumped over the bench. Grampy said he was surprised that we did not hear the Magistrate at our house, which was about a mile away. The Magistrate caught a glimpse of Rebecca in the lineup. She was under arrest for number writing. The Magistrate looked and yelled, "REBECCCKKA, what are you doing here?" The magistrate and Rebecca had attended school together.

Occasionally an avid politician would concentrate on the number writers. Usually someone would tip off the number backer and business was put on hold until the heat was off the number writers. I recall when the surveying team of police was staking out a major number backer. They knew everything about him. They knew his system. They knew that he held the numbers in the high ceiling of his living room on Moyamensing Avenue. They knew what color phone he used. Aha! They were ready for the raid. They did not take into consideration that someone on the side of the law had warned him beforehand. The headline in a Philadelphia newspaper that day was, "I Wonder Where the Yellow Went?" In the Philadelphia newspaper style, they used the words in an ad for toothpaste to indicate there was no evidence of a yellow phone. The yellow phone disappeared.

If someone in the neighborhood hit the number because of my prayers, they sometimes gave me a tip. I put the money into my cigar box. Cachinga! I always had an ample supply of cigar boxes. Grampy Brennan smoked King Edward's cigars. He said I should not confuse him with the Irish Brennan as he was from Brennan-on-the Moor. I said, "Okay?" I did not know on the Moor from Moore Street, which was one block away from our house on Front Street. Moore Street was where the Little Heaven Baptist Church stood. Mr. Byett was the minister. He and my Irish Catholic father often spent hours together talking. My father sat in his maroon, mohair easy chair and faced Mr. Byett. Mr. Byett faced the wall where a picture of the Blessed Mother adorned the wall. It portrayed her as a child. She had blond hair. I did not think of it then but she was from the Middle East. The picture had a little thermometer on the right hand side of it toward the bottom of the picture. The picture always reminded me of my sister Marie; that was the extent of it. I do not think the Blessed Mother would hit her little sister, if she had one. I do not think the Blessed Mother would then cry first, indicating that the little sister had done something to her; No, I do not think the Blessed Mother would ever do anything like that.

Mr. Haley, the undertaker, came to our house toward the end of each year. He would leave an entire carton of holy pictures for us to distribute among the family. I think we gave him more business than anyone in the neighborhood did. As he was leaving, he said to Aunt

Mary, "Hope to see you, soon." She did not like that. She thought he was after her body. My father tried to reason with her. He thought it was a courteous thing for Mr. Haley to say to Aunt Mary. My father did not think that Mr. Haley meant he was after Aunt Mary's corpse. After much discussion back and forth, Aunt Mary said, "Keep that man away from me." My mother told us that she thinks Aunt Mary is just peeved because she is not hosting the wakes anymore. We were now the hosts of the wakes. I always liked having the wakes in our house. We received preferential treatment. Uncle Sam Coarse had been the first corpse in our house since we owned it. Aunt Mary and Uncle Sam had hosted more wakes than The Black Widow, a name we dubbed to a woman who could not keep a husband. They appeared healthy and then in a short time they were no longer with us. The Black Widow usually had an ample amount of insurance on each one of them. Insurance is important. The Black Widow looked like Popeye's Olive Oyl; handsome men gravitated toward her. Once the Black Widow set her sights upon a potential husband, it was as if she cast a spell upon him. Some of them left wives and families in order to marry the Black Widow. An alleged victim's son went to the police. His father had been very healthy, enjoyed life and died thirteen months to the day after marrying The Black Widow. I have heard no more since that time. Maybe the Black Widow died. Maybe there was not enough evidence for the prosecution of the Black Widow. Aunt Mary had told me to leave the detective work to the detectives. I just could not help thinking that maybe I could have solved the case.

Grampy continued to tell me not to confuse him with the Irish Brennan. The only thing I knew about Ireland was that my paternal grandparents were Irish.

CHAPTER 3

My grandmother Mariah and four of her sisters arrived in America at Delaware and Washington Avenues in South Philadelphia. It was on a misty Holy Thursday morning in April 1885. They originally were from County Roscommon and then County Sligo, Ireland. The entire family had emigrated to England several years before Mariah, Maggie, Annie, Lizzie and Jenny immigrated to America. While the Dolan family was well off in Ireland due to ownership of properties including farmlands, when the potato famine struck Ireland in the mid 1800s, there was a backlash for decades. Ireland was devastated. We believe that the family had emigrated to England in order to seek a better quality of life. They were only collecting a stipend of the rents. Hardly anyone had any money in Ireland after the potato famine struck. There were ten girls born to Mary Duffy Dolan and John Dolan. One daughter, who was baptized, Coleen, died shortly after her birth. She had been their first-born. Agnes, who was the youngest, died at age ten. There were no sons. After my great grandparents died, the rents from Ireland were divided among the eight remaining daughters. Theresa, Bridget and Ellen stayed in England.

Prior to my writing this book, I had the facts documented about my ancestors. I viewed them as just cold facts in a manuscript of family ancestry. There were no emotions. My outlook has changed after getting started on this book. I am writing this book because I wondered how I could go on breathing after my son Franny died. When I went over the family history, I felt my great grandparents' pain at the loss of a child just ten years of age. I realized that my grandmother Mariah had lost a sister that she knew. I visualized a little girl of ten, who was named Agnes. I wondered if they called her Aggie or Nussie or some other nickname. I wondered if we had any similar likes or dislikes. I visualized her dressing up in her mother's clothing. I wondered if she liked to rub the fresh pillowcase on her bed for comfort like the one I did. I pictured her lying in her bed, half-awake, half-asleep, listening to the sound of horses' hooves on cobblestone roads. I visualized her looking like me, laughing and being as fun loving as me. Finally, yet importantly, I wondered how my great grandparents went on breathing after Agnes died. I received strength from them and was able to know the entire family as people. I saw the tragedies and the triumphs. I felt the faith that kept them going. I realized that we all have an inner strength connected to a universal spiritual force. I believe we need to tap into it by living a good life, by doing our best with what God has bestowed upon us.

Most of the family information came from Sister Margaret Mary Vasey, who was Ellen Dolan Vasey's daughter. Sister Margaret Mary was a cloistered nun on the Isle of Wight in the British Isles. She was only permitted to write at certain times throughout my childhood. She told us that one of the Dolans had witnessed the apparition of The Blessed Mother at Knock, Ireland. We were always under the impression that it was Mary Duffy Dolan, my great grandmother. We researched in order to find the name documented. Several family members went to the shrine at Knock, Ireland. The closest name we came to the actual visionary was Beirne. Even the spelling was different from our relatives named Burns. We think that is who it was. I know the nun on the Isle of Wight was not into making up stories. I know that some of the immigrant's names have been changed due to illegible immigration papers.

My grandmother Mariah said the trip to America was harsh. Unlike our WASP ancestors, who arrived on schooners, the Irish Catholics sailed to America on an over crowded ship, The Teutonic. The trip was cold and damp. Each of the Dolan sisters carried one piece of luggage, a small suitcase. Their personal items were kept in Ellen Dolan Vasey's house in England. They were kept in the room that belonged to Sister Margaret Mary, who was called

Maggie, before she became a nun. From time to time, the Dolan sisters in America would write to their sister, Ellen, who was called Nellie, to request something precious to them. It was never anything expensive, just something that reminded them of home and assured them that someone was still there.

Despite the harsh journey and the fact that my grandmother was a bit green from being sea sick, she stood at the railing of the big ship as it channeled into the Port of Philadelphia, Pennsylvania, at Delaware and Washington Avenues, in the Southwark district of South Philadelphia. I wondered how she felt when she was about to disembark the ship. I admired her courage. I wondered if she had any apprehension about immigrating to America. She did not have to leave her homeland. She wanted to explore a land where opportunities abound.

I recalled a poem by Henry Wadsworth Longfellow entitled Evangeline, which immortalized a notable increase in the Catholic population in 1755. Five hundred Arcadians who were exiled from their native land found refuge in Philadelphia.

    ೞೞೞೞೞೞೞೞ
In that delightful land which is washed
By the Delaware's waters,
Guarding in sylvan shade the name of
Penn the Apostle,
There from the troubled sea had Evangeline landed,
An exile,
Finding among the children of Penn
A home and a country.
    ೞೞೞೞೞೞೞೞ

My grandmother said that the foghorn sounded as The Teutonic entered the port. A tugboat tooted. It was not in the way of the great ship; it just wanted to welcome the immigrants that had been fortunate enough to make it. The sound of the foghorn was a signal for Mrs. McSweeney to throw her pink shawl around her shoulders and walk around the corner to Delaware and Washington Avenues. Mrs. McSweeney lived on the west side of Swanson Street, directly across the small cobblestone street from where Gloria Dei Church stood. It still stands today. It is the second oldest Episcopal Church in America. It is also called Old Swedes. An essence of spirituality prevails. It can be felt throughout the entire area. It is the oldest brick building in Philadelphia. Old Swedes puts a new light on rest in peace. The living and dead come together. There is a cemetery that dates back to the early 1700s. Many notables are buried there. The cemetery is still in use. Its "tenants" include sea captains, scientists, Revolutionary and Civil War soldiers, artists and ministers. There are ordinary people who just wanted to be buried in the close knit, strong community of Gloria Dei. These neighborhood people have experienced the beauty and charm of a garden like setting while in their mortal states. There were the fun times I remember as a child and young teenager. The fundraisers were held right there in the cemetery. They included music, food, song, dance and friendship. At Christmastime, there is a Santa Lucia feast. There is a procession. The young participants wear wreaths of lit candles on their heads while singing the various carols of both Sweden and America. The sense of history is everywhere. Models of the Key of Kalmar and the Fogel Gryp are suspended from the ceiling. They were the first ships that brought the Swedish settlers to America.

The ship models and chandelier were given to the church by Carl Miles, a noted Swedish sculptor. Hints of the Georgian style, which was common to Philadelphia building for most of the eighteenth century, can be seen in the building's symmetrical composition and in the Flemish bond brick pattern. The steeply sloping roof is reminiscent of Swedish churches. There is a 1903 Hook and Hastings tracker organ. The Swedish style baptismal font was crafted in 1731 in Philadelphia. It is one of the oldest fonts still in use. Gloria Dei was designated a national historic site in 1942.

I always liked to go there. It makes a statement, "Life and death are here and there is nothing to fear, we all get along just fine." In the early 1950s, I was sitting in my friend Betty's house on Little League Street, which ran east to west from Swanson Street to Front Street. I was sitting on her sofa when I felt something whoosh by me. The most relaxed feeling then came over me. I could have drifted off to sleep. I felt so light. I would never have put the events together, except, Betty came in from the kitchen. She told me she thought she saw a Revolutionary War soldier. It seemed as though he was coming home for dinner. The smell of the chicken soup seemed to please him. Strange, she asked. I told her that they had just reinterred the remains of Revolutionary War soldiers and some of their families from a discovery of graves they made when they were digging up around Independence Hall; some were reinterred at Old Swedes Cemetery. Maybe he just wanted to come home for dinner; maybe he heard about your reputation, I teased. My sister Marie is buried there in front of the day care center. Most of our family members are buried in Catholic cemeteries. Marie wanted to be buried in Old Swedes cemetery. It is very special. We use to hang out there as teenagers. We were welcome. We never caused any trouble. The Reverend John Roak's son use to hang out with us. We sang Do Wop and we danced the Jitterbug. We put on skits. I remember Bobby Morgan acting as a Hollywood director. He had a Stetson beige hat on his head. They were fun times. When I tell people we use to hang out in a cemetery, the first response I get is, "What did you do there?" We were in center city dining one evening when I related the story of Gloria Dei to my brother-in-law. He asked the usual question. I suggested we go there after dinner. He could then see Old Swedes cemetery and we could visit Marie's grave. After we went there, he commented how lucky we were to have had Old Swedes in our lives and he understands why Marie wanted to be buried there. Most of the gravestones around Marie's grave are neighborhood names. They are recognizable. They stand among the gravestones of many historic people from centuries ago. Some of the engraving has been worn down and cannot be read anymore. I still have a sense of awe when I go there. I visualize the sea captains and soldiers and wonder what they were like. I wonder if they had families waiting for their return. The sense of spirituality in the stillness overtakes any apprehension. I realize that there is something more out there in the universe. Something far more is out there.

A few years ago, I went to Theresa Lamina Saulin's house in South Philly. Frank Bochanski and Grace McDade Bochanski were there. Sis Lingo was there. We had so much fun reminiscing about Old Swedes. It was just pure, innocent fun. I can tell that is not the impression people get at first. Some of the responses are actually amusing.

My grandmother Mariah said it was a festive atmosphere when they arrived in Philadelphia. The rain did not materialize. She said there were Pilgrims pumping umbrellas and dancing. The ones that were not pumping umbrellas and dancing were playing musical instruments such as the saxophone, bass fiddle, coronet and banjo. Some were beating drums. There were some dressed as Native American Indians. They were chanting.

Mrs. McSweeney, who was a friend of the Muldowney family from County Roscommon, Ireland, was going to host the five sisters until they were able to get situated. She carried a sign that had Dolan printed on it. A group of people surrounded her. They sorted it out and she connected with the Dolan sisters. There was no need to hire a teamster to take their luggage around the corner to the McSweeney house. The teamsters were people who went to a livery stable and hired a horse and a wagon for the day. Sometimes they hired a team of horses, depending on what services they were providing that day. The teamsters have a different connotation today. The teams of horses for the hucksters have been phased out. However, the word teamster remained. They were a mainstay in America. They also served as taxis. The hucksters went around from street to street in order to sell their various wares. People did not have to go to the market in those days. The market came to them. The sounds of the hucksters selling their wares were a constant all day long when weather permitted. The iceman came early. Most people had iceboxes before refrigerators were available or too costly for them to own. A block of ice needed to be put in the icebox every day in order to keep the perishables cold. The ice went on the top part of the icebox, which had a door on top and a door beneath it. It was encased in a wooden cabinet instead of the porcelain of the refrigerators of the 1940s. I remember bringing friends into our house to show them our "Frigidaire" refrigerator, which was porcelain. It also was electric. We were able to keep fruits and vegetables crisp although the fruit did not stay around long enough to be concerned about it being crisp.

All day long vendors were heard selling their various wares. Get da oranges, five cents fer a dozen; big, juicy oranges. Bananas, bui (big) bananas, seven cents a dozen. Tomatoes, Jursey (New Jersey) tomatoes, four fer a nickel. The butter and egg man came from Vineland every Saturday afternoon to sell his dairy products. He was a heavyset man in his early fifties. He had a little pencil behind his left ear. He had a little pad of paper in his shirt pocket on the same side as the pencil. He was always in a hurry. He always had a pocket full of change; and constantly jingled it. It made him feel important. I liked that sound. I wanted a pocket full of change also, so I could jingle it. Clothes props, clothes props, two for a quarter. Jevetawater, gelvatawater or galvetawater, depending on the nationality of the vendor. It was bleach. Then there was Stockie. Stockie was an old man who looked like Santa Claus. He carried his wares in a little square wicker woven basket. He sang out, "Yi, yi, yi, yi, Stockie, you got the footsie, I got the sockie, yi, yi, yi, yi Stockie." The ice cream man came around. He sold vanilla ice cream in a tiny paper cup. One cup cost three-cents. He wheeled around a homemade cart that was wooden and glass. I remember it being white. He wheeled it up to our front window.

When I was growing up in the 1940s and 1950s, the horses and wagons were almost phased out. When Maria mentioned the Pilgrims to Mrs. McSweeney, it made Mrs. McSweeney laugh. She told Maria that the Pilgrims had landed on Plymouth Rock in Massachusetts. She went on to say they were not Pilgrims but Mummers dressed as Quakers. Mrs. McSweeney told Mariah that the Mummers could do parodies of the Pilgrims; that was part of their entertainment. However, on this particular misty April morning the Mummers were dressed as Quakers to welcome the immigrants to Philadelphia. Mrs. McSweeney told the sisters that they might see more interesting souls than the Pilgrims when they would be living with her and her son, Sean, on Swanson Street, directly across the small cobblestone street from Old Swedes Cemetery. She went on to say that, most people in the neighborhood see a Spirit now and then but usually keep the sighting to themselves. She added that people think they watch out for them. The Dolan sisters were to stay in Sean's room. He was her only child. Mr. McSweeney went out to buy some candy for Sean several years prior; he had not been seen or heard from since. Sean went to the basement while the sisters stayed in his bedroom. It was okay with him at first. He was left more to himself with the drink. He worked on the waterfront when work was available. When payday came around, he always stopped to treat himself. He came home that Good Friday evening in 1885. He was very adamant about how he would run the Great US of A if he were president. He said there would be chicken every Sunday.

When I was growing up there were often two chickens or more for supper and it did not have to be Sunday. Like clockwork everyday the chicken trucks drove south on Front Street. A few of the State Pen kids would jump the trucks, have boxes of chickens off of it and sold in time for people to have on their tables by suppertime. It took me a while to catch on when they were going around the small streets, just like hucksters, chanting, hot chicken, hot chicken. Of course, they did not mean cooked chicken. We were taught never to get involved with anything like that. My brother, Bobby, told me that he wanted to graduate from Penn State, not the State Pen. I suppose the Chicken Pluckers Gang was not around in 1885. Sean McSweeney thought that he would have to do something great in order to provide chicken for every citizen who liked to eat chicken. Mrs. McSweeney was in denial, big time. She told the Dolan sisters not to listen to his ramblings and off-key singing. She went on to justify that he stops at the candy shop after work on Friday. The sisters would listen and chuckle among themselves. They could retreat to their room if the singing became too outrageous before Sean McSweeney passed out from the sugar, which everyone knew was the drink. As his moods changed from the drink, so did his songs.

When he became morose, he sang his version of Danny Boy. Then he became daring and sang, The Wild Colonial Boy. He then became reflective and sang; Have you ever crossed the sea to dear old Ireland?

"Oh, Jaysus, he's daft," says my grandmother. "After that trek we just completed we are lucky our bodies, minds and spirits are still intact. You know he has never crossed the sea to Ireland or the British Isles or anywhere else. The only thing close to the sea that he knows is the Delaware River." It was a sign for the Dolan sisters to go to their room before they went out of their minds from the off-key singing of Sean's sugar induced mind, which everyone knew was the whiskey. All of a sudden on a Friday evening, Ireland becomes the paradise of the earth. The potato famine had wiped families out completely. Even though the Brits had captured the wild Colonial Boy and Danny Boy never made it back to stand on his loved one's grave; the drink told Sean that was the place to be, the songs to sing and the US of A would be better off if Sean was running things. The Dolan sisters went to Saint Philip of Neri's Church on Easter Sunday, just days after arriving in America. They felt at home and joined in the singing of the Mass and the special Easter Hymns. They already knew the Latin.

> Alleluia! Alleluia! Let the holy Anthem Rise
> Like the sun from out the wave,
> He has risen up in triumph
> From the darkness of the grave

Edward Caswall, 1814-1878, Music: St. Basil's Hymnal, 1889

O salutaris Hostia	O saving Victim, open wide
Quae caeli pandis ostium:	The gate of heaven to us below,
Bella premunt hostila,	Our foes press on from every side;
Da robur, fer auxillium	Your aid supply, your strength bestow.

Saint Thomas Aquinas, 1227-1274; tr. by Edward Caswell, 1814-1878.
Music: Samuel Webbe, 1740-1816

The Dolan sisters had been praying that the will of God would be shown to them. The sisters agreed that they would open some type of store. They had faith that God would show the way. They were surprised that He answered their prayers so swiftly. They knew one thing and that was that they could not bear the thoughts of another Friday evening with Sean. Their prayers were answered through an elderly produce salesman. God works through people.

Easter Monday was a beautiful, sunny, Spring day. The teamsters were out in full force selling their various wares. The knife sharpener was the first vendor they heard. Next, was the produce salesman. My grandmother went out to buy some produce. She struck up a conversation with the elderly gentleman, who was running his business that day by going around from street to street in order to sell the produce. He knew names that my grandmother recognized from County Roscommon and County Sligo, Ireland. He had immigrated from Ireland several years prior. He told my grandmother that he was the operator of a produce store on south Front Street. He told her that because of the lack of business over the winter, he was going to operate his business by going around from cobblestone street to cobblestone street when the weather permitted. My grandmother told him that the Dolan sisters were looking for a place to start a business. After discussing it among themselves after Mass on Easter Sunday, the consensus was that they would go into the candy business. They knew how to make Irish potato candy topped with cinnamon. The stipend that they received from the rents in Ireland would pay the rent on a little store. The gentleman told her that he would talk to his landlord, Joe Rodgers, who owned the store. Joe Rodgers was a kind man, who owned much of the property in the area of Front Street between Tasker and Morris Streets. Like the Dolan sisters, Joe was only collecting a stipend of the rents, if any, due to the tenants lack of money. Mariah said that they would surely pay the rent, as they know what it is like not to be paid the rents; and besides they were honest people. The gentleman told her that he would be returning the horse and wagon to the livery stable at Front and Tasker Streets around five p.m. He told her that he would clean up, have a bite to eat and then go to see Joe Rodgers. The produce salesman's house was located in the alley next to the livery stable. I always liked those little houses in the courts. They looked like little cottages in Ireland. Aunt Mary showed me pictures of Ireland. She had been the beneficiary of her mother Mariah's collection of pictures. Unlike one of the other courts on the same block, that particular court had indoor plumbing.

Mariah mentioned the conversation to everyone in the house. They began praying. The Dolan sisters always had a pair of rosary beads in their hands. However, on this beautiful Easter Monday, even the candy-loving son of Mrs. McSweeney was praying. He had given up his room to the Dolan sisters and now he would like to have it back. He thought it was a good idea at the time; he soon grew tired of it.

Mariah went about her business for the day almost forgetting the conversation with the nice gentleman who was selling produce. Sure enough, at seven o'clock that evening, a knock came on the McSweeneys' door. Sean opened the door and admitted the gentleman into the house. He told Sean his name was Anthony Boyle. He told Sean that he originally was from County Roscommon, Ireland. He asked to see Mariah. Sean announced that a suitor was there from her region in Ireland. Mr. Boyle told Sean that he was not a suitor. Sean then announced that the gentleman was not there to court her, too bad.

When Maria heard the Anthony part, she said that Saint Anthony never fails to find things for them, never. The sisters had been making a novena to Saint Anthony. They petitioned him to ask God to help them find a business, and he did.

Mr. Boyle told Mariah that the store would be available to them. It just so happened that the people who were living in the apartment above the store had just moved out. Thus they would be getting living quarters as well if they so desired.

They arranged to meet Joe Rodgers at the store the next morning. They arose early. When the story was related to me by my father or Aunt Mary, I visualized them looking like Louisa May Alcott's Little Women. The Dolan sisters were dressed in their Sunday best. They all wore hats. Mariah's hat was dark green and had a band of lighter green. It also had brown plumes and feathers adorning it. The other sisters wore hats of different colors but none as ornate as Mariah's hat. They walked west on little League Street. They walked one block north in order to see Sparks Shot Tower at Front and Carpenter Streets. They had heard about the various shot towers that were built in America. Sparks Shot Tower was the first one built in America. It was built in 1808. The tower made musket balls along with other ammunition. It was used during the war of 1812. It is a classic of American architect. It still stands today. There is also a recreation hall on the site. Many of the various high schools benefit from the basketball players that learn to play basketball at Shot Tower. The sisters walked all around it and then turned and headed south on Front Street toward their destination.

Joe Rodgers was waiting for them. To their surprise, the store was immaculate. It was shined and polished and had glass cases in it. Since Joe owned several stores, he was able to take needed equipment from one place to put into another. The glass cases were decorated with little white paper doilies awaiting the particular dishes of candy that would sit atop each of the doilies. The sisters had their miniature Irish tea set with them and proudly placed it atop a shelf on the wall behind the glass cases that held the candy. It was Tara China with little green shamrocks throughout each piece.

One thing was clear to the Dolan sisters; if they wanted more supplies, a couple of them had to go to work outside of the store. My grandmother, Mariah, obtained a job at Saint Theresa's rectory on south Broad Street, in South Philadelphia. Lizzie obtained a job at the Annunciation rectory at Tenth and Dickinson Streets. Within a few years, the Dolan sisters had married. Mariah, Lizzie and Maggie chose to live in the neighborhood of Southwark. Aunt Annie went to Riverside, New Jersey, to live. I have such fond memories of the quaint little town of Riverside. The industry is on the waterfront, the rest of the town is as quaint as a New England town. My sister, Marie and I use to go there for a week or two every summer. We stayed with the Olgiotti family. Sis was our age. My grandmother's sister, Annie, was her grandmother. We went to the movie and then went to the restaurant next door to the theatre. We ordered tomato pie and Tak a Boost. I liked that sugary, syrupy drink so much. Part of the reason was that it brought my blood sugar up quickly. I know now that was part of the reason that it made me feel so good, I did not know it then.

Aunt Jenny moved to the Neck section of South Philly. The Neck section of South Philly is where the Mummers are believed to have originated. They were originally called New Year Shooters. It is believed that it came from a Swedish custom; that is before it took on a life of its own. There are various accounts. One account remains clear; people dressed in costumes, shot guns, banged pots and pans, played musical instruments and welcomed in the New Year with great revelry.

I liked to go down to the Neck section where Aunt Jenny lived. We crossed a small wooden bridge to go over to Aunt Jenny's house. We passed huge sunflowers. Aunt Jenny had a wooden house with a small wooden porch on the front of it. We had plenty of protectors around when we were growing up. The eligible grandsons of the Dolan sisters had served in World War II. I had plenty of my own family over there protecting us from the mad dictator's scheme. Two did not return. They were killed in action.

During World War II, the parodies that were done on the mad dictators gave people a sense of togetherness. The Mummers had hung Hitler four years in a row in the New Year Parade. Patriotism prevailed. It gave us hope, courage and the knowledge that we were all in this war together. The Mummers played music reminiscent of World War I, such as: We did it before and we can do it again. Oh boy, Hitler, Mussolini and Tojo, watch out. It is time to kick butt.

World War II songs prevailed; Let's remember Pearl Harbor, Praise the Lord and pass the ammunition, When the lights go on again all over the world. There were so many, a song for every situation. We were troopers both over there and on the home front.

Life had not been easy for most immigrants, but they were tough and served our country well.

CHILDREN AT PLAY
OLD SWEDES CEMETERY-

Sparks Shot Tower-Front and Carpenter Streets
Philadelphia, Pa.-

CHAPTER 4

My grandmother had many tragedies in her lifetime. She had lost a child at birth. She also had suffered the loss a nine-year-old daughter, who was named after her deceased sister, Agnes. My grandfather died when my father was only six years of age. There were little if any social programs around to help widows. My grandmother continued to operate the candy store with her sister, Maggie Dolan Veasey. Times were rough for everyone. My father's brother Eddie was killed in an accident on the waterfront of South Philly. It involved a horse and an ice wagon. Eddie was nineteen years of age. My father then needed to leave school in the fourth grade; he needed to go to work in order for his mother and himself to survive. The nuns at Sacred Heart of Jesus taught my father well in those four grades. He had the most beautiful handwriting of any that I have ever seen. It was like calligraphy. He went to a livery stable as a child of nine and usually obtained a job for the day helping one of the many teamsters deliver their wares. If work was not available at a livery stable, he did something else. He was willing to work. He knew he had an important mission of being the man of the house. He was ingenuous and would have made a good veterinarian had circumstances permitted. He loved animals; he would tend to any who came into his path. At times, he would patch them up in order to get them back on their feet. However, he was lucky if he made enough money to keep body and soul together. He always took care of his mother. She was making next to nothing in the candy store. He related a story to me about one Thanksgiving

Day. He told me that he saw a sign in the butcher shop window. It advertised, "Turkeys, twenty five cents." Oh boy! He thought he would work extra hard that day and buy a turkey for his mother. When he got the quarter together, he went to the butcher shop. He asked for a turkey and held up his quarter. The butcher told him it was twenty-five cents a pound. My father could not afford a turkey; therefore, he bought a pound of scrapple for ten cents. He gave his mother the other fifteen cents. They sat down to a scrapple dinner on Thanksgiving Day that year. I always felt like crying when he told me that story. He usually told it as we were about to have our Thanksgiving feast of turkey with filling, cranberries, mashed potatoes, corns, peas, cole slaw and gravy. There was always a tray of celery, carrots, olives and other fresh vegetables as well. When we were called to dinner, my father told Bobby to go around the corner to Aunt Mary's house, in order to escort her to dinner at our house. My mother did not like that. She and Aunt Mary silently locked horns. Mother says, "She never brings a pie." Daddy says, "Here, take my dinner to her." I went to pick up his plate; I was smacked across the hand. Bobby was already on his way to escort Aunt Mary to dinner. Aunt Mary was already waiting for him, although she was never formally invited. The ritual was tradition. We always had an ample supply of pies. Horn and Hardart, the automat restaurant, also sold holidays pies for take out. I liked their mincemeat pies. Bobby liked the apple pie. We had about six different varieties of pies. Now why in the world would we need another pie? However, tradition is tradition. Aunt Mary now lived in the same house that my father had bought for his widowed mother when he obtained a steady job for the City of Philadelphia. He and his mother had lived together until my grandmother died shortly before my parents were wed in January 1932, on a Wednesday. My parents lived there for a short while before they made an upwardly mobile move to Fernon Street, which was about eighty yards around the corner from where Aunt Mary now lived on Mountain Street. Aunt Mary made sure the lock on her door was secure. She then closed the door. The door to our house opened and Bobby escorted Aunt Mary to the dining room. He took her coat and carefully placed it on a hanger inside of the closet. He held out the chair for her to sit at her regular seat at the dining room table. Daddy then said grace. We said grace at every meal. It was so festive with the lit crystal chandelier in our dining room. We had a very large table so we did not need to extend it. We used the extension board for another seat at the table. We put it between two chairs. My mother put an Irish Linen tablecloth on the table. Aunt Mary's Waterford crystal glasses held a glass of ice water for everyone. The silverware had been shined and polished the week before Thanksgiving and set methodically at each person's place. We had Christmas music playing softly in the background from the RCA (Radio Corporation of America) record machine. John McCormick sang his version of Bless This House.

The turkey smelled so good. We were sneaking out into the kitchen pulling off little pieces here and there, before it actually adorned the middle of the dining room table. I liked to eat pieces of the crisp brown skin. My father always ceremoniously cut the turkey. We then passed our plates to him in order to have him place our order of turkey. I liked the drumstick. The rest of the food was passed around for all to take an ample supply. We laughed and had fun. Daddy did not relate anymore of his lost childhood. Aunt Mary was the oldest of Mariah and Edward's children, daddy was the youngest. They were the only two who were still around. My mother always had guilt about his poor childhood. She did not realize that it was not her fault.

My mother and father were wed at Our Lady of Mount Carmel Church, at Third and Wolf Streets in South Philly. My mother wore an elegant bridal gown with an attached veil that trailed five feet behind her. Their three feet by four feet picture as a bride and groom adorned the wall for all to see when they entered our living room. It was in an ornate bronze frame and covered a huge part of the wall on the same side as the front door. It made a statement; everything is legitimate here.

My mother looked like the Queen of England (Queen Elizabeth) and had the airs about her like the Queen herself. Upon returning from their honeymoon at Niagara Falls, Canada, they began their life together in the cozy, little house that my father owned on Mountain Street. Everything was there; all my mother had to do was bring her personal items. My father did all of the work in order to make it palatial for my mother. He wallpapered all the walls and performed some cosmetic work on the quaint little colonial American style brick house. The "Queen" was pleased. The two bedrooms and bathroom upstairs were perfect for a starter home. Although it was tiny, it was elegant. My mother picked out the various designs for the wallpaper. There were bouquets of small yellow roses in the master bedroom. Aunt Mary always made novenas to Saint Theresa, The Little Flower. If she saw the yellow roses, she would know for sure that it was a sign from The Little Flower. She would know that the little saint had heard her novena and will do her best to get Aunt Mary's request granted.

The bathroom was decorated in aquamarine. It had a tub with claw feet, a toilet and a washbasin. The walls did not have designs; they were plain aquamarine. My mother selected the curtains that would adorn the window in the bathroom. The curtains were pure white. The shades underneath the curtains were also pure white. Ah, life was good until the Queen discovered that almost every house on Mountain Street had an outhouse and not an indoor plumbing bathroom like their house had. Oh, it was not that realization alone that preceded the move, although the part about the outhouses always made me laugh. I could not even picture the Queen of England using an outhouse, not that she would have to if she lived in my parents' house on Mountain Street, in South Philly.

The people on Mountain Street were meticulously clean. People used lime in the potties of the outhouses. They also cleaned with a disinfectant. The fire hydrant was turned on often in the summertime. The water ran down into the brick gutters of Mountain Street. That was okay with the Queen. One hot summer day the hydrant was turned on legally with the sprinkler attached. A City employee turned it on with the special wrench that they used. It was kept on for a short while. It was a kindness to give the people relief from the dog days of summer. More often than not, someone who had a wrench that worked to open the fire hydrant turned it on illegally. My mother observed entire families either going under the sprinkler or simply getting their baths from the water that was flowing down the brick gutters from the water spewing from the hydrant. They brought their Lifebuoy soap, washcloths and towels. I personally thought that necessity is the mother of invention. However, the Queen was appalled. She was not pleased. She told my father that they would have to move. Therefore, they did. They moved approximately eighty yards away, around the corner to Fernon Street where I was born in 1934. My mother thought that it was a much classier street. Some of the houses on Fernon Street had outhouses; however, the people of Fernon Street were never seen washing in the spotless gutters of Fernon Street. It was definitely an upwardly mobile move.

My sister Marie was born on December 7, 1932 in that little house on the corner of Fernon and Hancock Streets. Most babies were born in their own homes in those days. A midwife assisted with the birth. Sometimes the doctor arrived on time; sometimes the doctor arrived after the birth. The doctor did arrive before Marie's birth and was there to give her a good smack on her behind. She did her best to earn it while we were growing up together. Overall she was a protective sister, even though she dubbed me "little twerp." When I was two years of age and she was four years of age, we were at our aunt's house. I brushed up against an ornament. My aunt yelled at me. Marie did not like that. She said, "Come on hon. We're going home." I do not think Marie even knew where home was. My aunt picked me up and told me that she did not mean to scare me. She was afraid the ornament would break and I would get hurt. Marie took off her coat and then removed my coat and we stayed until my mother picked us up.

My father was advancing rapidly in his job with the City of Philadelphia. He had a good, secure job. He had advanced to Foreman, a title that encompassed many of the City departments. His job included overseeing the Stables, Streets, Automobiles and Construction Departments. He also tended to the animals that would come his way. I liked the stable at Ninth and Dauphin Streets. Marie and I rode horses there. Sometimes, the Bargas twins went with us. Marie fell off the horse one day and would not go again. I fell off one time. I let Mr. Bargas cuff his hands in order to enable me to climb back onto the horse. My father's job was much like a middle management job. He liked to work with the horses. If they appeared lethargic, he would rub them down with an ointment. He also served as a blacksmith for them. If a stray animal came along, he usually brought it home. I remember him asking my mother if she would mind if he brought a puppy home. They could not locate the owner. My mother told him it was okay with her. When he arrived home the next evening, he had the largest Dalmatian dog we have ever seen. He stayed for a while and then he went to live with Aunt Jenny down the Neck section of South Philly.

Daddy was also very liberal in inviting nuns to our home. The only problem was that he did not tell my mother beforehand. The Poor Clares stopped by to use the washroom. Sometimes on washday, the bathroom floor was full of clothes that my mother was sorting out. She had a wringer washing machine. My mother had been sorting the wash. Sometimes the washer leaked oil. She made sure that the piles of clothes were not near the oil. My mother would almost become hysterical when the nuns showed up to use the bathroom. I doubt if the Poor Clares cared about the oil or clothes on the floor. They were just relieved to have a place to go. The Poor Clares went around the neighborhood from door to door for donations. Almost everyone gave them a coin or more. They did good works with the money collected. They helped the homeless and the downtrodden and anyone who needed help.

Like most of the Irish Catholic family men, my father always offered his services to the Sacred Heart of Jesus parish, which was his home parish. He also was devoted to Saint Theresa of Avilla parish and Annunciation parish. The latter two being where my grandmother and her sister had worked. I remember my father soaking jars in order to get the labels off them for Annunciation parish. They in turn redeemed them for classroom equipment. My father became very friendly with Father Kelly and Sister Marie Liguori. We considered Sister Marie Liguori our aunt. One windy day at Annunciation, something happened to the flagpole that stood high above the school. My father volunteered to climb up the pole in order to get the compromised flagpole stable again. Sister Marie Liguori started ranting and raving to Father Kelly. She said, "Do you know he has a new baby at home, do you know he has two little girls besides the new baby boy, do you know that?" She would not let up on Father Kelly. He finally responded, "I will climb up the flagpole and give him absolution." She said, "No, we will pray." Therefore, they did and daddy returned safely to the ground, having fixed the compromised flag. My father could do anything. He was endowed with many gifts. He could build a house if he so desired.

Sister Marie Liguori became a frequent guest at our house. The Poor Clares continued to stop by in order to use the bathroom and maybe have a bite to eat. Mother continued to get hysterical if it was washday and clothes and oil were on the floor. Daddy continued to bring stray animals home. Marie rolled me around in the mud of our back yard. My white dress, white shoes and white stocking became dark brown. I laughed. I was not a whiner. My mother told me to stay there. She would get the hose and spray me down. She then brought out a washcloth, towel and a cake of Lifebuoy soap and washed me with it. <A>; I thought that was what inspired the move to Fernon Street in the first place? That was over two and one half years before I was born. Maybe she had thought it over, and concluded that necessity was the mother of invention.

CHAPTER 5

My mother typed a little book on the events of my birth. She read it to me before I went to sleep. When I started to understand, it opened up a world of interest in people, belief in God and the diversity of humanity.

My mother told me that Doctor Enders had predicted I would be born on December 7, 1934, the same exact date that my sister, Marie, was born two years earlier. {Oh, how sweet! However, I knew I would never go for that. I wanted my own birthday. It is tragic enough that I had to be punished because Adam and Eve ate an apple that the Lord said they should not eat. I already had one strike against me, Original sin. If they did not get me to the church on time to be baptized in the name of Jesus and I died, I was then to go to a place called Limbo for all eternity. Moreover, to boot, I never even had a taste of the apple. You bet I kicked up a storm over the possibility of having to share my birthday with my sister, Marie.} Mother went on to say that God kept in touch with them by giving them signs that I was going to be sent to them earlier than Doctor Enders had predicted. That is how God communicated with us she told me. Sometimes He would give us a thought, at other times; He would send us a feeling. Then, He started to send sharp pangs in my stomach; sometimes it felt as if I was being kicked in the stomach from the inside. {I was kicking up a storm.} Mother said it was a very tumultuous feeling. They thought it best if Mrs. Parker came a day early. Mrs. Parker was the midwife. She stayed for an entire week after the birth. She cooked for us, dusted and took care of all your needs while I rested for a week. She also fed Billy. Billy was a stray goat that came wandering into the City stable at Ninth and Dauphin Streets in North Philly. Daddy was the stable boss. He brought Billy home after being unable to decipher who owned him. Billy stayed in the yard. The yard was dirt. After a rainstorm, all we could see were Billy's eyes. Billy was pure white with a little spot of black on his forehead. After a heavy rain, he became all black with little spots of white showing on his eyes. She then informed me that when Billie would baa, I would be fed or coddled.

{A goat! I was getting attention when a goat would baa! Read one of those baby books, Mother. That story is not good for my self-esteem.}

Two days before Christmas in 1934, I was taken to Sacred Heart of Jesus Church to be baptized. She said I was to be named Joan Helen Morrisroe. After considering the name Clare for a long time, they decided on Joan. The Helen was after my grandmother, Ella May Rittenhouse Brennan. Helen is derived from Ella in Latin. Clare is a very beautiful name, however in our neighborhood; too many names for me could be conjured up from it. Saint Clare of Assisi would become, Saint Clare, the sissy, or instead of all clear when the cops passed by the crapshooters, it would become, all Clare. It could go on and on depending on what type of disposition little Clare would have. I always thought Joan was a very good choice at that particular time in that particular neighborhood. It conjured up thoughts of Saint Joan of Arc, dressed in armor and leading an army to victory. I did not think anybody would be messing with Saint Joan of Arc. I did not realize initially that she would have to lead an entire army and <linalittin> fight until she was captured. I did not know initially that she was burned at the stake. I learned that later in second grade at Sacred Heart School. I stilled liked being named after the great little <topalowoagan> warrior.

Mother said that she would not be accompanying us to the church for the baptism. She said it was custom for a new mother to stay at home and prepare for the christening party. She told me that she had already been churched on December 16, 1934. Being churched was a ritual where a new mother knelt at the altar rail after the last Sunday Mass and received a special blessing. Despite the prediction that I would be born on December 7, 1934, the same date my sister, Marie, was born two years earlier, it did not work out that way. I had my own birthday. My mother told me how that came about.

Snow flurries had been predicted for the evening of December 6, 1934. God thought it best if His special deliveries were started at the stroke of midnight. He thought He would send you early on December 6, 1934. Because babies were born in their own homes in our neighborhood in 1934, He had to give the angel precise directions. The angels were very bright and seldom made a mistake of delivering a baby to a widow in our neighborhood. Very rarely did that happen; however if it did the widow would accept the baby and relate to people that the baby was conceived by the Holy Ghost. {Oh, boy, another puzzler for me. I later learned in Bible history studies that only Jesus Christ was conceived by the Holy Ghost who is now The Holy Spirit. The bible thinks that Christ was the only one conceived by the Holy Ghost who is now the Holy Spirit.} The angels were very cautious in locating the people who were waiting for the delivery of a baby. He said you were to be delivered to Mary and Andrew Morrisroe. He gave the angel our address on Fernon Street, in the great historic city of Philadelphia. He described the tiny house. He said it was so warm inside. There were Christmas carols in the background. They were being aired through the little 1934 Philco radio. There was much laughter and love. The combination of scents and sounds in the house could be displayed as a Charles Dickens Christmas Carol.

Because it was shortly before His birthday and He was sending a special delivery, He decided to send a gift of His own, that is, besides you. He selected a little angel who would accompany the tall elegant angel that was to bring you from heaven. The little one was to take her place on top of the Christmas tree until the feast of the Magi, January 6, 1935. He placed a wreath of holly on the little angel's head. He placed a little pink bow on the tiny angel's head. The tall blond angel wore a blue sash. She had delicate arms and hands. Her feet were just as delicate and she wore no shoes. When you arrived safe, she was to stand beside you to light and guard, to rule and guide you until the day God calls you back to heaven. Your guardian angel left a little prayer card for you. It was a petition for her to help you as she was always there for you. She likes it when you talk to her in your prayers.

Oh Angel of God,
My guardian dear,
To whom God's love,
Entrusts me here,
Ever this day be at my side,
To light and guard,
To rule and guide.

Guardian Angel from heaven so bright,
Watching beside me to lead me aright,
Fold thy wing around me, and guard me with Love
Softly sing songs to me of heaven above.
                                    Amen.

He then told them that even though they were angels and usually did not eat food of mortals, the mincemeat cookies that Mrs. Parker had baked would be difficult to pass up by angel or mortal. He gave them permission to eat Mrs. Parker's mincemeat cookies with the secret ingredient, if they so desired. He then looked you over one more time; put his finger under your nose to the top of your lips that left an indent that denotes, inspected by Number One. He then said, "Be off, I will be watching over you." They started the flight at the stroke of midnight on December 6, 1934. It took them exactly one hour and fifteen minutes to arrive and have you in my arms by one fifteen a.m. Dr. Enders and Mrs. Parker were there. Mother said that I did not cry when I received the traditional smack on my behind. {I was so happy that I did not have to share my birthday with my sister Marie. It would have really been difficult to cry when I was getting my own birthday December 6, 1934, the day before my sister Marie was to celebrate her second birthday.} We always had our own birthday party. Our relatives came to both parties.

The little angel was placed on top of the tree by my guardian angel. She was so tiny and cute. Mother said she reminded her so much of me. She smiled a lot.

Aunt Mary and Uncle Sam arrived at our house at two p.m. That was the time that we ate dinner on Sundays. The practicing Catholics in our neighborhood usually attended nine or ten a.m. Mass. Many then stopped at Lipsky's bakery at Fourth and Moore Streets for fresh baked kosher rolls. They would then be served with eggs, bacon, ham or sausage. Scrapple is a Philly favorite that was often served as well. Scrapple is delicious to most people in Philadelphia. Visitors we have had from other parts of the country usually decline it. It can be served at any meal. I just try not to read the label. The kids in our neighborhood who did not like scrapple simply said, "Don't skeve me out." Sometimes pancakes would be served; however, the pancakes never stopped anyone from eating Lipsky's rolls or bagels as well. People ate until they were stuffed. It was almost noon. The morning ritual was complete.

Uncle Sam held the door open for Aunt Mary to enter our tiny, cozy house that Sunday afternoon. Aunt Mary was dressed to the nines. She always wore a big hat. Her hat was adorned with bows and a bird feather or two. It was deep purple. Hats were fashionable; and besides we needed to wear hats when we went to church. Aunt Mary was a big woman, about five feet, eleven inches tall. Aunt Mary was crippled. She could not bend her right knee. She had an accident on her roller skates when she was eleven years of age. Her entire kneecap was torn open. It was stitched up without having the bones set; therefore, that is why she could not bend her right knee. However, when Aunt Mary got dressed to the nines she presented a regal image. She always wore gloves and carried a fashionable handbag made of genuine leather. Aunt Mary had so many sage Irish sayings that would hit the nail right on the head.

Aunt Mary was carrying a beautiful yellow box from Strawbridge and Clothier Department Store. It contained my christening ensemble. The gown was long and pure silk. It had lace on the collar and cuffs. The front had three little laced trimmed buttons. The hat matched. It was pure silk and lace as well. The christening ensemble was as white as snow.

When Aunt Mary removed her coat, my father carefully took it and placed it in the cellar way, which served as an entrance to the cellar as well as a closet. Aunt Mary kept her hat on her head. She then sat down and observed the surroundings. She looked at the Christmas tree, which was kept lit all day that Sunday. She said, "I swear that little angel on top of the Christmas tree has put on weight." My mother and father thought that was funny. How could a little angel on top of a Christmas tree put on weight?

Shortly after their arrival, everyone sat down to dinner. Mrs. Parker served the dinner before taking her seat at the dining room table. She was not staying consistently with us anymore. She thought the family would need some help on the christening day. She served roast chicken with roasted garlic potatoes. Daddy always liked to feed Aunt Mary potatoes, as Aunt Mary was still upset because of the potato famine that had struck Ireland in the 1800s. Mrs. Parker also served glazed carrots and a salad. The salad dressing consisted of oil, vinegar, ketchup, herbs and spices. Everyone liked her cooking. Those who still had room for dessert topped off their meal with cannolis, an Italian pastry, bought at the Reading Terminal Market, not far from Philadelphia's City Hall. Tea was then served. My mother never tasted coffee. Tea was served in our house. Mother liked it with lemon; daddy liked it with milk, both added sugar. Aunt Mary drank coffee in the mornings. She took it with canned milk only, no sugar. Uncle Sam delivered it to her room service style. When Aunt Mary and Uncle Sam came to our house, she drank tea. Uncle Sam passed it up. It was now three p.m. The baptism was scheduled for four p.m.

After dinner, the table was cleared immediately. It was then converted into a dressing table. A soft white towel, the size of a crib sheet was put over the mahogany table. Mrs. Parker put the various items that would be needed on the newly converted dressing table. There were baby powder, diapers, diaper pins and my entire christening ensemble. There was a beautiful gold cross and chain.

Aunt Mary decided that the kitchen sink would be the best place to bathe me. She would not have to bend her knee that was unbendable because of the roller skating accident that she had when she was eleven years of age. It worked out well, as the kitchen was still warm from all the cooking that was done for dinner. Mrs. Parker also had a humongous batch of her famous mincemeat cookies in the oven. She was preparing them for the christening party.

Aunt Mary gingerly wrapped me in a soft snowy white towel and dried my tiny body thoroughly before sprinkling the baby powder on me. I smiled when I smelled the powder. It made me smell like a little rose bud. The rose essence emitting from my tiny body served to enhance the smells, sights and sounds of Christmas on that Sunday afternoon on our house on Fernon Street, in the great historic City of Philadelphia.

While Christmas carols were sounding in the background, the decorative bells on our front door were ringing. Someone was at the door. Who could it be? Mrs. Parker opened the door and welcomed Mr. Bargas, who worked with my father. Mr. Bargas was a colored man, with a very laid-back disposition. Mr. Bargas was dressed in his Sunday best. He wore a brown suit with a Stetson hat to match. His shirt was as white as the soft towel Aunt Mary used to dry me. They suspected that his bright yellow tie with brown stripes had been an early Christmas present from one of his loved ones. Everyone was happy to see him but a little puzzled why he was at our house at that time of the day. He and his wife Bessie had new twin daughters. They were born on Thanksgiving Day, 1934. One was named Pricilla and the other was named Prudence. The only way they could be distinguished from one another was that Pricilla had a white toe. It was the big toe on her right foot. The twins looked as if they had basked on the beach of heaven for a week before God inspected them. Pricilla may have had something covering her big toe on her right foot. Most likely, the number one inspector let it be. That way the Bargas family would be able to tell them apart as they were identical in every way. Since Pricilla had a white toe on her right foot, the same baby would not be fed repeatedly while the other one starved to death.

Mr. Bargas winked at daddy and said, "Ready Andy?" Daddy replied that he would be ready in a short while. He invited Mr. Bargas to have a seat. Mr. Bargas sat across from the Christmas tree. He observed the surroundings. Mr. Bargas said, "That tree looks even more beautiful than it looked on December 6, the day Joan was born." That was when Mr. Bargas stopped by with daddy's Christmas bonus from the City. He then commented, "It looks like that baby angel on top of the tree is putting on weight." Strange, two people in one day thought that the little angel was putting on weight.

Daddy asked Mr. Bargas if he would like to join him for a cup of tea in the living room. That way they would not get in the way of my baptism preparations. Daddy brought Mr. Bargas the tea in one of our best China cups that was trimmed with pink baby roses. The entire house smelled so cozy, it made it conducive for someone to doze off right after a meal. There were the various smells from the pine, spruce and baby powder among other scents emitting from the kitchen. The smell of Mrs. Parker's mincemeat cookies with the secret ingredient was emitting from the oven.

Aunt Mary thought that the prominent rose smell was from Saint Theresa, The Little Flower. Aunt Mary had been making a novena to the little saint. It was the sign that Aunt Mary had been waiting for. The Little Flower was working on Aunt Mary's request. The request had to be for the greater honor and glory of God. Aunt Mary derived a conclusion. The scent of roses from the baby powder and now our best China cups adorned with tiny pink roses were sure signs that Saint Theresa would try to obtain Aunt Mary's request. There was no doubt. The sign always came before the request materialized.

The pre-baptismal ritual was almost complete. Aunt Mary put my little white silk shoes on my tiny feet, over long white stockings. It crossed her mind that maybe she should have gotten a larger size. I put on weight rapidly. She put the long white christening gown over a long white silk undergarment. She then put the tiny silk and lace hat on my head. She wrapped me in a soft white blanket edged in silk. She then put a shawl around me. Simultaneously, the dressing was complete and Mr. Bargas had finished his tea and another of Mrs. Parker's mincemeat cookies. He grinned from ear to ear. My mother told me that she had her eyes focused on me when she heard, "Oh, my goodness, goodness gracious." She looked out the door, as she thought it started to snow or something was out there that prompted them to echo in harmony, "Oh, my goodness, goodness gracious." Glory Be! Sitting right outside of our tiny house on Fernon Street was the most beautiful, polished, largest automobile that they have ever seen. It was fit for the mayor himself to ride. It could be used to pick up dignitaries when they came to town. It was a cream-colored car. It had gold tone fenders. It had a highly polished front grill topped by a huge chrome hood ornament. It had a chrome bumper in front with a vertical chrome bar extending down the bumper on each side of the regal car. It was a 1935 Cadillac LaSalle. The tires were whitewalls and the wheels had shiny chrome spokes. There was a chrome running board on each side of the car. The running boards were so wide that people could stand on them if necessary. Aunt Mary proclaimed, "That is the most beautiful machine that I have ever seen." Aunt Mary always called automobiles machines. She was especially happy because it served to make it easier for her to enter and exit. That enhanced the regal appearance that she always presented.

Uncle John held me while Mr. Barges helped Aunt Mary enter the car. Mr. Bargas opened and closed the door of the royal carriage. He was extremely careful with it, as he had signed it out from the City's fleet of cars. After inspecting the royal coach that was to be driven to Sacred Heart Church by Mr. Bargas, the neighbors closed their doors and went inside their houses in order to prepare for the christening party that was to be held at The Gallagher New Year Association Club.

The majestic car pulled up in front of the Sacred Heart of Jesus Church. Heads turned. The royal baby was inside. The godmother, Aunt Mary, was bedecked like a Queen from head to toe. She gingerly held the precious cargo. Uncle John, the godfather, alighted from the great LaSalle Cadillac. He took me from Aunt Mary until her ritual of getting out of the car was complete. Daddy followed them up the steps of Sacred Heart Church to the two wooden doors, carved with an architectural design that was from a bygone era. Mr. Bargas followed daddy in order to hold the elaborate doors open for the pre-christening entourage to pass through. Mr. Bargas went into the church to show his respects. He then went back to the royal coach that he had signed out from the fleet of City cars. It even had a heater. He waited out there for us. He put his head back and relaxed while he enjoyed Latin hymns and carols being sung by the choir. They were practicing for the Christmas Masses.

ৡৡৡৡৡৡৡৡ

It Came Upon the Midnight Clear
That glorious song of old,
From angels bending near the earth
To touch their harps of gold;
"Peace on the earth, good will to all
From heav'ns all gracious king"
The world in solemn stillness lay,
To hear the angels sing.

Edmund H. Sears, 1810-1876, alt, Music: Richard S. Willis, 1819-1900, alt.

Mr. Bargas, who was a Baptist, remarked that the sights, sounds and smells that day made him feel like he was in heaven. He then touched the steering wheel and the horn blared. It was a very unusual day. When Mr. Bargas blew the horn of the brand new Cadillac LaSalle; he began to think of the song, Blow Gabriel Blow. Mr. Bargas and his family, Bessie and the twins, Prudence and Pricilla went to New York in the beginning of December 1934. His ninety-four year old grandmother lived there. She was fragile now. They wanted to make sure she that she saw the twins before Gabriel blows his horn for her. They took a tour of the town and noted that Broadway was producing, "Anything Goes." Cole Porter wrote a song entitled, Blow Gabriel Blow, for the musical. The music was blaring all over Broadway. It was a catchy tune and carried a very strong spiritual message. Mr. and Mrs. Bargas had wished that they could have seen the show; however, they had the twins with them at all times during that visit with Granny Bargas. When they returned from New York, he knew the tune from Blow Gabriel Blow. He remembered some of the words. He aligned it with his life, as he was known to have strayed a little from his Baptist upbringing. Of course, it was when he was sowing his wild oats. He started to sing his own version of the song, Blow Gabriel Blow by Cole Porter. He waved his arms and sang. He began to reflect on his own life and thanked God for all the blessings that had been bestowed upon him. The choir practicing for Christmas Mass inside of Sacred Heart Church served to enhance the spiritual feeling that Mr. Bargas had that day. The carols permeated the air that day. Occasionally, he tooted the horn in order to know that he was not dreaming.

Aunt Mary paused at the middle altar where Jesus was hanging on the cross. She extended her arms outward toward Jesus while she held me. I was like a royal princess in the royal palace of Jesus Christ. The church was bedecked with Christmas trees and greens. There was a Nativity stable under Saint Joseph's altar, to the right. The red and white poinsettias adorned the altars. The poinsettias and greens were professionally placed on the altars by the florists of The Little Flower Shoppe. The linen altar cloths were placed on the altar first. Mary Frost tended to the linens on the altars. She did it with pride. When I became old enough, I helped her, as did her nieces, Margie Walters, who was in my class and Ellen Smith, who was a few years younger than we were. Mary was a saintly person who had something inside of her that was rare and precious. Most of the good people I know have it; however, Mary expressed it. Her response was always, "Oh, sweet Mother." She loved doing the linens for the altars. We passed the Blessed Mother's altar on the left side of the church in order to go to the alcove where the baptismal font sat. Aunt Mary stepped down into the alcove. Aunt Mary said I smiled throughout the entire baptism until the priest put salt on my tongue. She told me that I did not like that and let them know it by crying. It was a short-lived cry. {Do not make any waves, kid; you have your own birthday.}

When the baptism was complete, the entire entourage including Father Gatens proceeded to the Blessed Mother's altar. Aunt Mary handed me to Father Gatens. He then proceeded to dedicate me to the Blessed Virgin Mary. The choir began singing Ave Maria in Latin.

Father Gatens placed me on the Blessed Mother's altar and asked her to watch over me all the days of my life. He dedicated me to the Blessed Mother. He then pinned a little gold miraculous medal on my christening gown. He then handed me back to Aunt Mary. Aunt Mary adjusted my blanket and shawl so I would be cozy and warm when we went outside. The entourage then proceeded to the main altar. They paid their respects to Jesus and headed to the right side altar, where Saint Joseph's altar stood. The manger was set up under his statue. Everyone took a piece of straw from the manger. It was tradition that if a person carried a piece of straw from the manger, they would never be without money during the coming New Year. The choir was now singing "Silent Night." They practiced it in both English and Latin. The cultural arts were all there in that little church. All the pomp and circumstances were there. Mr. Bargas alighted from the car and opened the door in order for the passengers to enter. Uncle John held me while Mr. Bargas was assisting Aunt Mary into the car. Uncle John then handed me back to Aunt Mary and entered the car. He sat next to Aunt Mary. Daddy sat in front on the passenger's side. Mr. Bargas then closed the door of the majestic car.

Mother told me that something very unusual happened after we left for church. She continued, to this day we are not exactly sure what happened with the little angel on top of our Christmas tree. We have pieced it together to the best of our knowledge. Uncle Sam was nodding off on the right hand side of our maroon, mohair sofa, which was very conducive to dozing after a Sunday dinner. It was so comfortable. Mrs. Parker was straightening up our tiny house. She had completed putting all the paraphernalia from the pre-baptism ritual away. She put the rose scented baby powder, the diapers and pins neatly in the buffet drawer. She stored your little pink bathtub under the kitchen sink. She went to the living room where Uncle Sam was dozing. She straightened the ornaments on the tree. A few ornaments had been disarranged. There were many people in that tiny house on that Sunday afternoon, December 23, 1934. Then she noticed the little angel. She was not on the spire of the tree. The little angel had fallen from the spire of the tree to the branch below. She was sitting down on the branch. She seemed to be playing, "This little piggy went to market" with her toes. {Mother then started to play, "This little piggy went to market," with my toes.} The baby angel was grinning from ear to ear, a silly little grin. Then she turned green. Mrs. Parker thought that the reflections from the Christmas ornaments and the Christmas lights were causing the little angel to turn green and then red also. Mrs. Parker thought she would ask Uncle Sam to put her back where she belongs. She then went about her business of dusting and straightening up the house. She checked the tin cookie box that had a scene of snow and sleds. People were happily riding in them. The scene on the lid of the cookie box enabled her to visualize the people in the sleigh singing, Jingle Bells, Jingle Bells.

To her amazement, there were no cookies in the tin box. She pondered and thought it strange. Nobody was downstairs but her and Uncle Sam. She did not eat them and Uncle Sam was dozing. She knew he did not eat them. Her stirring around the living room awakened Uncle Sam. He hazily rubbed his eyes and nodded off again for a few seconds. In a few minutes, he became fully awake. He saw Mrs. Parker standing there. He looked at Mrs. Parker as if she could give him an answer. The question was unknown. He told Mrs. Parker he had a dream. He said that it seemed so real. He added that he must have eaten too much for dinner. He told her that the dream was lingering. Mrs. Parker was all ears. She listened intently as he related his dream. He told her he dreamed that two angels flew through our living room window. They were dressed in toga like robes that had red sashes, which had him wondering if they were archangels. They each had a heavenly glow about them. He went on to say that the angels were about the size of baby Joan's guardian angel. Each had blond hair with wings as soft as lambs' wool. The beautiful angel on the right gently lifted the little baby angel that came down from heaven with Joan. If he did not know it was a dream, he would swear that he heard the beautiful angel on the left talking to the baby angel. The angel told the baby angel that God wanted her to come back home until she got a little older, maybe age seven, when she would reach the age of reason. That really puzzled him, as he knew the age of reason was seven; however, he did not think it applied to angels. He went on to say, there are many things about heaven and earth that we do not know. He paused, smiled and said that it was only a dream. Anything can happen in dreams. The tall angel on the left had a very melodic voice. It did not sound as though she was chastising the little baby angel. She went on to tell her that the reason God wanted her to come back home was that she could not stop eating Mrs. Parker's mincemeat cookies, the ones with the secret ingredient in them. God thinks there are some things you still have to learn. The little angel was grinning from ear to ear. As they were flying back out of the window, the little one gave him a wink and sent him an angel kiss. He thought gee, I wonder what the secret ingredient is. As if that smaller baby angel was reading his mind, she mouthed the word, LOVE. He then heard the most beautiful Chrismas carol being sung. Mrs. Parker said <A> indeed, as if she was putting the pieces of a puzzle together. She ran to the window. However, by now they were out of sight. She did hear the Christmas hymns. They seemed to be permeating the heavens and earth. It was a very unusual day. Mother said that when she came downstairs from preparing for the christening party, they told her the story about the angels. They searched and searched. They opened doors and drawers. They looked behind furniture and the most obvious, behind the Christmas tree. There was no sign of the little angel. Mother then went to the front door and opened it, causing the bells to jingle. She heard the strains of Brahms lullaby. She smelled incense. She saw no sign of the angels. A feeling of contentment and spirituality came over her. She knew that they did not have to look for the baby angel, she just knew. She closed the door, and then opened the lid on the cookie box. She ate one of Mrs. Parker's mincemeat cookies before she left for the christening party.

BABY JOAN CIRCA 1935-

The door of the Gallagher New Years Association was opened in anticipation of the arrival of the christening party. It was thirty-five degrees outside on that Sunday, December 23, 1934. There were so many people inside waiting for us that the cold did not matter. The royal carriage pulled up in front of the Gallagher Club. The Mummers honored me by playing, Baby take a Bow. Every third or fourth song at a Mummers' congregate is "Oh, Dem Golden Slippers." The Fisk Jubilee Singers originally sang the song. James A. Bland had it published in 1889.

Oh, my golden slippers are laid away,
Kase I don't 'speck To wear 'em till my wedding day,
And my long tail'd cat I loved so well,
I will wear up in de chariot in de morn,
And my long white robe dat I bought last June,
Ise gwine to get changed kase it fits to soon,
And de ole grey hoss dat I used to drive,
I will hitch him to Chariot in de morn

Oh, dem golden slippers, Oh, dem golden slippers!
Oh dem golden slippers, ise 'gwine to wear,
because dey look so neat
Oh, dem golden slippers!
Oh, dem Golden Slippers ise gwine to wear,
to walk de golden street.

● ● ● ● ● ● ● ●

Almost everyone strutted when Oh, dem golden slippers was played. A Mummers Strut is unique to Philadelphia. When a person performs the Mummers Strut, it is as if they are being transformed into another dimension. It releases cares and woes. This is evident in watching people do the Mummers Strut. It indicates that they do not take themselves too serious, if only for the duration of the strut.

I think every psychiatrist should teach a person The Mummers Strut, have them perform it and then come back to talk to the doctor.

Mary Ellen Lord was already at the club with my sister Marie. She was our baby sitter. Her best friend, Anna May McGuire, was with her. My cousin, Nuny Wootten, who was eight years of age, took me in her arms while Aunt Mary was taking off her coat. Aunt Mary never took off her hat. She did not have to worry about looking silly doing the Mummers Strut. She was crippled and she did not dance. All of our relatives were there.

To this day, no one can figure out exactly what went on with Billy. A little elf came into the party with Billy on a chain. He took Billy over to Aunt Jenny and then the elf vanished. Aunt Jenny took Billy home to her little farm down the Neck section of Philadelphia. It was too far away from our house to hear Billy baa, thus I was not fed or coddled when he would baa. It was a most unusual day.

People danced into the wee hours of the morning. It was now Christmas Eve. The door to the Gallagher Club closed and people returned to their homes to prepare for Christmas.

Mother said that a knock came on our door around one p.m. on Christmas Eve. It was Aunt Blanche, who owned the Aunt Blanche Card Shop on south Second Street. She said that she would sit with Marie and me if they needed to do some shopping or last minute chores. Aunt Blanche had been a cloistered nun before she left the convent. She was a good soul but a little eccentric. They thanked her and told her that they would be delighted if they could go to Aunt Mary and Uncle Sam's house on Front Street. They had a Tara China Nativity set for them. It lit up. Someone had brought it back from a trip to Ireland. They mentioned to Aunt Blanche that Aunt Mary had been making a novena to Saint Theresa, The Little Flower. They went on to say that, they thought Aunt Mary's request was going to be granted because of all the rose sights and smells that have been sent. Aunt Blanche said, "Oh, really, I'm happy the Little Flower is listening to someone. I am so angry with Saint Theresa, that I turned her picture to the wall. Everyone would know that I was snubbed by her, Protestants and Catholics as well."

Aunt Mary and Uncle Sam were delightfully surprised to see them. They loved the Nativity set and were happy to have it in time to light it for Christmas Eve.

They mentioned how kind Aunt Blanche was to offer her services to baby sit. They also mentioned that she was very angry with Saint Theresa, The Little Flower. They told Aunt Mary the entire story. Aunt Mary said, "Oh really." I feel like going up to that little shop and putting Saint Theresa's picture back to the dignified position it deserves. Aunt Mary ranted and raved over the disrespect Aunt Blanche had shown to The Little Flower. They then knew Aunt Mary's request to Saint Theresa had been granted.

On New Years Eve of 1934 daddy translated and then wrote down all the orders for Chinese food. It was tradition in our family to go to China Town and bring the Chinese food home for the family. Aunt Mary hardly pronounced anything proper in English, so when it came to Chinese, she named a few new dishes for them. Daddy knew what she meant and ordered the dishes as listed on the Chinese menu. If he had ordered them by what Aunt Mary was calling them, they would have started talking back to him in Chinese. My mother's fortune cookie read, "Before the end of the year; you will be receiver of great news." At midnight, everyone came outside their homes and banged pots and pans or blew horns. They then returned to their homes and closed their doors.

During the summer of 2006, I had the pleasure of visiting with Mary Ellen Lord McNasby and Anna May McGuire Szmborski. They were in their eighties at the time. They had been lifelong friends. My niece, Marie Oxenford Hicks, went with me when I visited Anna May. We sat together for several hours. Marie was doing a genealogy on the family. We had pictures with us. Anna May knew where they were and what they were called. She identified my grandmother's candy store and told us exactly where it had been located on south Front Street. The candy store had been torn down before I was born. Some buildings had deteriorated under the high pressure of the wind and rain off the Delaware River. She identified a store on the southeast corner of Front and Tasker Streets. She told us it had been a restaurant called Fennesseys. She pointed out a sign that was in the window of the restaurant. It was an advertisement for a Topps beer making kit. I asked her if she knew where the Speakeasy had been on Second Street. She told me exactly where it had been. I told her about the Speakeasy story. My mother barged in one Sunday when daddy was drinking beer and gave him an ultimatum, "The family or the drink. You are Irish and you can't drink." The bartender remarked that she was worse than Slop's wife was. Daddy told her that he would be home shortly as were his plans. He never did go into the Speakeasy again. Daddy would get sick whenever he drank; it made him melancholy and remorseful. He also had a nervous stomach. There was no drinking in our house growing up; maybe that is why people thought we were rich.

We had so much fun recalling odd people in our neighborhood. The woman who lived next door to Anna May always wore one woman's shoe and one man's shoe. She told someone who dared to mention it that it was an Irish custom. Aunt Mary never heard of it. The woman was buried in one woman's shoe and one man's shoe. Then, there was the cat lady. She had cats all over the house. They covered every piece of furniture including the dining room table. She had a round hole cut out in her front window so they could go in and out. We found a stray cat and thought that since she liked cats so much, we would put the cat in her window. About one hour later her door opened and the cat was put out. She knew all her cats. There must have been one hundred at least.

ɪ́ ɪ́ ɪ́ ɪ́ ɪ́ ɪ́ ɪ́ ɪ́

Anna May mentioned my christening party. She said it was so festive and so much fun. She remembered everybody. We interchanged information, some I already knew from being told by my mother.

By 1934, we could have formed our own League of Nations. My Aunt Nellie was there. She was married to Uncle Doc Markette. His name was really Frank, but everyone called him Doc. He was very proficient at making Dago Red wine. My cousins, Anthony, Eddie and Buddy Markette were there. The entire clan of the Brennan-on-the Moor was there. The Old Lady was there. Even though

Grampy Brennan was very prim and proper, that is all he ever called his stepmother, The Old Lady. Aunt Alice was there with young Alice who was four going on five. My cousin Jack Mooney was there. He was two going on three. He was already a little Mummer. In the 1950s, a magazine, which was a supplement to The Philadelphia newspaper, carried a story about three generations of Mooneys being Mummers. John Sr, who was Uncle John's father, my Uncle John, who was John Jr. and my cousin, Jack, who was John III were on the cover. The Gallagher Club was filled to capacity for my christening party. Aunt Winnie was there with my cousins, Jack, Mike and Joe. My Uncle John, who was my father's brother, died two months before his son Joe was born in January 1934. He was thirty-two years of age. Mary Olgioti, who was my father's cousin, was there with Charlie, her husband, Sissy Mary, and Charles, their children. Even though Mary was my father's age, we simply called her Mary. We called her husband Charlie. Charlie was Italian. Mary's sister, Annie, was there with her husband Dippy. Dippy was Polish. My cousins Margaret, Elaine and Kate were there. They called Elaine, E lane. I was the only one who ever mentioned it. It conjured up images of a product being in the E lane of a store. Elaine Dadino and I often had a good laugh at that and some other events that we experienced together when she came over to Philly from Riverside, New Jersey. All the Woottens were there: Aunt Mame, Uncle Dick, Eddie, Margaret, Sis, Anna, Lizzie, Richie, Jimmy, Sammy and Nuny. Nuny was the youngest. Aunt Jenny McGonigal was there.

The original Mummers or New Year Shooters were not organized when the Dolan sisters arrived in America. Some came out dressed as Quakers, who Maria thought were Pilgrims. Just a few years after that, there was a clash between two clubs at Second and Federal Streets in South Philly. One Mummer was killed, the reason, booze and jealously. Shortly after that, it was organized with prizes given by the City of Philadelphia. "Who came in first?" always echoed throughout South Philly on New Years afternoon.

Uncle John contributed much to Mummery and served as president of the Mummers Association in the 1950s. The capes were so elaborate that they needed to be held down by pageboys;

sometimes twelve pageboys were needed. They were paid one dollar each.

When I go to other parts of the country, hardly anyone knows of the Mummers. It is an extravaganza, a work of art. I hope to see it televised nationwide one day. I think that will happen. I never met a person who does not know what the Mardi Gras is. The Mummers need to be recognized as well. It is a tradition that dates back centuries. It is an integral part of Philadelphia, Pennsylvania.

GALLAGHER CLUB CAPTAIN'S CAPE CIRCA 1955-

CHAPTER 6

The New Year Shooters strutted down "2" Street on January 1, 1935, despite the official parade being postponed due to a prediction of snow and sleet. The Fancy Clubs did not march. Neither rain, nor snow, nor sleet, nor hail could prevent the Comic Clubs from marching. Tradition was that people in our neighborhood would open their doors to the New Year Shooters. The original New Year Shooters were served pepper pot soup. We served bean soup. If they were drunk and rowdy, they did not get into the house. The early groups of New Year Shooters costumes and participants often were quite crude, before The New Year Associations came into being. It had been custom to hold masquerade balls on New Years Eve. Their lady friends joined them and danced throughout the night into the wee hours of the morning. Custom was that after the ball was over, they would then go to the farmhouses in the Neck section of Philadelphia for breakfast. The Tin Pan Alley first platinum song hit in American music history Charles K. Harris's "After the Ball" in 1892 became one of the songs that the revelers sang. Everyone knew the chorus.

> After the ball is over
> After the break of morn
> After the dancers' leaving,
> After the stars are gone,
> Many a heart is aching,
> If you could read them all
> Many the hopes that have vanished
> After the ball.

❤

{It did not sound like a very happy New Year to me; everybody had a broken heart.}

After daylight, they would return to the downtown streets that were below Cedar Street, which is now South Street. It remained east of Broad Street. On January 1, 1901, when the New Year Association was official the Mummers marched in an organized parade. It was an all male extravaganza. There were female impersonators here and there but not in the String Band Division. The earlier clubs had supplied their own marching music. Long before that, they employed professional military bands or fife and drum corps.

A few days after New Years Day, the early clubs would hold "cake cuttings," for which some sold tickets. All present would eat their full of cake and wash it down with liquids of various potency. After many years of these impromptu but exceedingly colorful New Years celebrations, the City of Philadelphia officially proposed and put into action the idea of a mammoth parade on Broad Street including all the Clubs need to have permits. With this centralization and the City of Philadelphia taking an official part, clubs from other parts of the city took part. On January 1, 1901, the first-combined parade was held on Broad Street starting at Porter Street. Porter Street is three miles south of City Hall. The parade officially ended at Girard Avenue, one and one half mile north of City Hall. That year the parade was over shortly after the noon hour, when the various clubs returned to their respective districts for their time honored parade of single units. "2" Street is where most of the clubhouses were situated. The "2" Street parade continued sometimes into the wee hours of the next morning.

The contesting for prizes became a real contest with City authorized cash prizes. The prizes hardly covered the costs of the elaborate capes and costumes, but it was being recognized. Besides, the Mummers would have gone on spending their own money for all of the equipment including the price of the costumes. It was in their blood. Money cannot buy the enthusiasm and pride. The day after the parade is over for one New Year, the Mummers start rehearsing for the parade for the next year. The first-combined parade consisted of a number of Fancy Clubs, quite a few Comic Clubs and a couple of String Bands. The beauty of the settings and the improvement in the type of costumes has lifted this parade into an extravaganza. We've come a long way, baby! Females have participated in the parade since 1975 in The String Band Division. When my Uncle John Mooney told us, we were elated. One of the young ladies was a musician at Hallahan High School. Her name was Maryjean Maahs. They were not marching in the Gallagher Club. They marched for the Crean String Band. Hallahan is my Alma Mater. My sister Marie also graduated from Hallahan High School, the first all girls Catholic High School in America. We were proud. Go, Mickey, Go! Mickey Mouse is Hallahan's mascot.

The Comic Clubs present a parody on all the events that had occurred in the previous year. It continues today.

As if our little Philco radio was sending subliminal information, when I studied 1935 in World History it all sounded familiar to me. Franklin Delano Roosevelt was using the various letters in his fireside chats. The SSA (Social Security Act) provided pensions for the elderly, unemployed and the handicapped. The WPA (Works Project Administration) employed workers to hospitals, schools, parks and airports. It also enabled work for artists, writers and musicians.

Bruno Hauptman was convicted of kidnapping the Lindbergh baby. My mother said she did not think he did it. She thought he was the patsy for it; however, my mother did not use words like patsy, because she acted like the Queen of England. Her British heritage was evident in her remarkable image of the Queen.

The drum was beating slowly in the background. It would be six more years before the beat hit us. The Nazi party repudiated the Versailles Treaty. They introduced compulsory military service. Mussolini invaded Ethiopia.

In March of 1935, Lookie, Lookie, Lookie, here comes Cookie was the number one song on the hit parade. There were so many little girls called Cookie in 1935 that almost every class in Sacred Heart School had a Cookie in it during the 1940s. There were Cookie Hesser, Cookie Nickels, and Cookie Cook; oops, that would have evolved anyway even if the song were not around. The prediction in my mother's fortune cookie from New Years Eve of

1934 did evolve. It predicted that my mother would receive great news later in 1935. Well, lo and behold! In October of 1935, Dr. Enders predicted that we would be getting an addition to the family. The baby was born at the end of July 1936. My mother named my brother Robert Andrew. We called him Bobby. She liked the name and besides that is what I called my doll baby. I think I was trying to say baby. I thought that Bobby was lucky. He could have been called Bartholomew, which my mother had in mind. I cannot even imagine the image that it would have served to conjure up in our neighborhood. It is a very nice name; however, I think too much could have been in the offing for a nickname he may not have liked. Of course, Bobby's birth necessitated a move to a larger house. Shortly after my brother's birth, we moved to a three-story house on Tasker Street in South Philly. I began to form my own memories in that house on Tasker Street. I can still visualize the green cellar doors that opened from the outside of the house. When opened there were four steps that led down to the cellar door. I do not ever remember using it for an exit or entrance but I suppose it was like that for a reason when the house was built. We had a coal-fueled heater. The coal man would arrive with a ton or two of coal. It was then funneled down into the coal bin. The funnel looked like a sliding board. The heater needed to be fueled with the coal. The heater needed to be banked. That simply meant new coal had to be added and the ashes needed to be taken out with a shovel. The ashes needed to be put out by the curbside once a week. There was an ash day. The ash men would take them away. It was a very warm house. We had hot water type radiators.

We received a big bonus from living in that house. Atmore's mincemeat factory was a few doors away on Tasker Street. Trucks pulled in several times a day to deliver apples. To be good neighbors, the manager of Atmore's mincemeat factory left the gate open so the children could take apples. Bobby just loved apples, more than anyone I ever knew.

Aunt Mary and Uncle Sam lived on Front Street. We were permitted to go to their house, which was less than a block away, if someone crossed us on Fernon Street. Aunt Mary was the closest person to a grandmother I ever had and I loved Aunt Mary. She had sage Irish sayings or just Irish sayings that befuddled me until I became old enough to understand them. Aunt Mary also had some information that I do not know from where it came to this day. She warned me not to walk on the Chinese pavements on Second Street. There were two Chinese laundries on the 1500 block of south Second Street. She said they would come out, snatch me and keep me. I would then need to iron shirts. You know I deliberately went out of my way to avoid walking on those pavements. I did not want to live with the Chinese. Besides, I did not know how to iron. Aunt Mary warned me about the Gypsies on South Street. She said they would pull me in and keep me. They would make me wear long golden earrings and teach me how to read a crystal ball. Then if they wanted to take me on a Gypsy caravan, they would do so. I never walked on the dirty store front windows where they lived. I crossed the street. Danger was lurking all around at home and abroad.

Hitler was a maniac who had high ambitions of conquering the world. He wanted an Aryan nation. He exterminated Jews and Gypsies. The handicapped and dumb were targeted. Anyone who did not fit into Hitler's dictatorial scheme was targeted. Father Maximilian Kolbe gave his life so a family man may be set free. He is now Saint Maximilian Kolbe. Out of the group of starving people selected, four survived. Finally, after four days, they were given injections of cyanide. The saintly priest was one of them. The Jews lost over six million people to the holocaust. When I watch survivors of families that were exterminated by the Nazis, I wonder how they went on, how some are still here to tell their stories. They appear lucid and not raving mad. They have lives like other people. I believe the human spirit is connected to each one of their loved ones who were victims of the mad house painter turned Chancellor. Their stories must be told. The holocaust must never be forgotten, never. History must never be forgotten. Most of the tragic events of history are documented, including all the wars and slavery. The holocaust also is documented and immortalized. Some are denying it.

The chaos of the Great Depression enabled the dictators to rise to power. The Japanese had seized Manchuria. Everyone was busy trying to eke out an existence. That is when the evil dictators struck. It is incomprehensible how a crazy man could rise to power and saluted like a God. Heil Hitler was the mantra. The right arm was extended outward and the Swastika was on the left armband of the khaki colored uniforms or any of the clothing that members of the Nazi Party wore. There were Nazi youth groups that followed in the adults footsteps. Heil Hitler! We did not learn about the concentration camps or exterminating camps overtly. Stories were leaking out. I heard people saying Hitler is making soap and lampshades from human skin. I thought that was a bizarre thing to be doing even for a crazy man. I also thought that the people had died first of natural causes. I did not know about the gas chambers and the horrific, unfathomable conditions that the targeted people were subjected to from the maniacs.

On New Years Eve of 1936, daddy went to Chinatown to get our traditional Chinese food. Of course, Aunt Mary always ordered yok a may, sometimes she ordered, Chop Sue. It sounded as though she thought the Chinese were giving an order for a girl named Sue to chop something. She never wanted a Pu Pu platter or any of the Moo Shu dishes. She never ordered a dish with a general's name in it because she was not sure on whose side he was. She did read the fortune cookies and thought the predictions would evolve. Usually they were so general that the prediction could apply to anyone. In the course of one year, there are surprises, good fortune and anything that a fortune cookie would predict.

While we were eating our Chinese food, the little Philco radio was playing the top ten songs of 1936. I especially liked Pennies from Heaven. Whenever it rained, I would go outside and look for the pennies to be falling between the raindrops. Aunt Mary said it doesn't rain real pennies. It means if life is tough, eventually it will bring good out of bad. Of course, it did not apply to the mad dictators. They were unreasonable. Unbelievable!

In 1937, I was allowed to sit outside with some playmates. I was two and one half years of age in the summer of 1937. We were to live on Tasker Street until the day before my fifth birthday, December 6, 1939. My friend Anna Muldowney had moved to Front Street. I was relieved because I would know somebody. Actually, it was only yards away and I already knew everybody, East, South, North and West of the four-block radius of our neighborhood. Aunt Mary lived in the house we were to move into in 1939. In 1938, Aunt Mary broke her good leg. My mother made her lunch every day. She delegated Marie to deliver it to her. I was allowed to go, as Marie was six and had friends who were seven, accompanying her. Marie did not like that and called me the little twerp in front of her friends. One summer at noon, we headed to Aunt Mary's house with a platter. It contained bologna, potato salad, cole slaw, bread, pickles, olives, tomatoes and lettuce. When we reached Ford Brothers machine shop, we discovered a potsy game already drawn on the sidewalk. Ford Brothers machine shop made new parts or repaired old parts for the various ships that pulled into and out of the ports on the Delaware River. Marie told me to hold Aunt Mary's platter while she did hopscotch. She was handing it to me and tossing the pebble into the chalk lined game simultaneously. Oops! There goes Aunt Mary's bologna. I put it back on the platter, but she would be able to tell. It had little pebbles in it. She would say we were doing monkeyshines. She must have thought we were related to Tarzan, because she always called my brother Bobby, Boy. I crossed Front Street; no cars were coming. I went up the court where the little Trinity houses stood. The name evolved from the layout of the houses. There were three stories, with one room on each floor. This particular court had two stories. They still were called Trinity Houses in our neighborhood. Four stood on the left side of the alley. Four stood in the back of the alley, which was the court. The outhouses were lined neatly in a row in a far off corner of the court. I never had been to Ireland, but I always visualized the court looking like residences in Ireland. My babysitter's grandmother sat outside the picket fence of their little house. She was blind. I asked her if I could use her spigot. She said, "Yes, Joanie." She said I was a good girl and very clean. Then she asked who crossed me. I told her I had a crew of friends watching out for cars so I could cross. She said, "Okay, be careful crossing back over." I told her that I would. Then I thanked her and left. In the alley part of the court where the four other houses stood, my father's cousin, Johnny McDonald was sitting outside. Johnny has lost his left eye in World War I. He was a hero. I stopped and talked to him. I made sure that I stood on his left side, so he could not see the bologna I was holding. He asked me who crossed me. I told him.

He said, "Be careful crossing back." I told him I would do that. The bologna went back on the platter and Aunt Mary never knew about the monkeyshines.

Marie, Joan and Bobby Morrisroe

Trinity Court -2007-

CHAPTER 7

In 1939, the winds of change were evident all over the world. The war that broke out in Europe soon spread around the world. Over forty-six nations were the Allies against the axis powers. This included the United States. Despite America trying to stay neutral, most Americans knew that war was brewing all over the world. I did not know it. Because all those letters that Franklin Delano Roosevelt was spewing from our Philco radio gave me enough on my mind trying to figure them out. I heard some letters that I thought may benefit me. I especially concentrated on The FDIC (Federal Deposit Insurance Corporation). I thought that when I fill my cigar box with money, I could then safely deposit it in the bank of my choice. It would have to say FDIC insured for sure. My mother had told me about the Great Depression. She told me that she had worked for a stock brokerage firm by the name of Montgomery Scott on that infamous day. She went on to say that, some people had lost all their money in the stock market crash, which was the start of the Great Depression. She said some people who had lost all their money were opening windows and jumping out onto the pavement below to their deaths. She told me they could not bear the thoughts of not having money and all the luxuries that money could buy. They were now penniless after the stock market crashed on Tuesday, October 29, 1929. They could not even rationalize life without maids, chauffeurs, big fancy cars, silk suits and shaving lotion that smelled of success; shaving lotion that would cost an ordinary working man his entire week's wages. My mother went on to say that, she could hear the sounds of despair echoing eerily before a window was opened and someone jumped to their death. She said she sensed they did not have faith in their lives, the type of faith that believes that everything will work out eventually, the kind of faith that heals one's soul and the belief that new opportunities will open up despite having to go through some hard times. I started thinking, what would I do if I opened my cigar box one day and it was empty? I wanted to test my faith before anything like that happened, of course. I thought it out and could not even bear the thoughts of not trusting God. When someone entered our house on Front Street, a picture of The Sacred Heart of Jesus spelled out the ground rules. It adorned our wall on the right side of the vestibule. It was a picture of a handsome Irish or English looking Christ lovingly looking out at us. It was not one of those pictures of Jesus that made me feel guilty before I even did anything wrong. The picture of Jesus had an inscription beneath it.

†

Christ is the head of this house
The unseen host at every meal
The protector of the family
ຣວຣວຣວ

Now they were the ground rules. Of course, in Western movies, I had seen different versions of ground rules. I noticed signs on the bar or hotel rooms that laid out the ground rules, which included no spitting, no cussing, no leaving without paying and no gun slinging. There were others of course but I did not exactly know what was going on upstairs until I was older. In addition, most saloons mandated that the cowboys' horses be tied up outside and not brought inside the bar, which always had swinging doors. There were no vestibules out West. They probably did not need the little hall that served to scrape the weather off the cowboys' feet or to put a wet umbrella in a stand that stood in a vestibule. Their little porches served the purpose. I never did witness a cowboy, black or white hat bring their horse into the bar. That was a ground rule, "No horses inside the saloons." Everyone knew that. However, right here in the City of Philadelphia in the early 1950s, my cousin Mario brought a horse into the auditorium of Southeast Catholic High School for boys. Oh, boy! It would have been gun-slinging time if it were out West. Southeast Catholic High School for boys did not even allow the boys to wear certain type of shoes. They took pride in the auditorium and the wooden floor was always impeccably polished. That <amintschiuchsowagan> act of disobedience did not go over too well with the powers that were. Mario was expelled immediately. He never did return to school. Years later, he married a millionaire and did not need that education in the long run. You see, God does close one door and opens another. It just was not to be the door at Southeast Catholic High School for boys.

The Westerns had such an impact on our lives, that we would actually sit on the rug-covered floor of the Lyric Theater on a Saturday afternoon to see the next sequence of how the good guy or gal escaped the perilous situation that they had been in on the previous Saturday, before the announcement, "To be continued." I liked Tarzan and The Perils of Pauline. The latter being more nerve wracking; as they would announce, to be continued next week just as Pauline was about to be run over by a train. You bet I would sit on the floor if a seat was not available. Someone always came along to rescue Pauline. It reminded me of what I was taught about having faith.

When television came along later in the 1940s, we named the bar diagonally across from our house on Front Street, Frontier Playhouse, after a popular Western. On a Friday evening, we could kneel on our couch and see one or two of the stevedores flying out of the Frontier Playhouse, to continue the fight outside. Two brothers who were six feet tall usually were the first ones flying through the bar doors. The sheriff arrived in the form of a tiny woman, their mother. She would somehow grab each by an ear and take them home. They went like two little lambs. Hooray!

In March of 1939, we received another addition to the family. He was named Andrew Joseph Morrisroe, Jr. In August of 1939, Meyer Harris who lived next door to us on Tasker Street committed suicide. Mrs. Harris, his mother came into our house screaming. My mother went into the house with her. My baby sitter, Mary Ellen, said she did not think my mother liked that. I can attest my mother did not like that scene. From August of 1939 until December of

1939, we lived outside as much as possible. We had family in the neighborhood with which we could visit or just run in to use the bathroom. When weather permitted, we went to Feldman's Drug Store at Fourth Street and Snyder Avenue for milkshakes. Drug stores always had soda fountains with stools. We sat in a booth. Aunt Alice and my cousins, Alice and Jack went with us sometimes. The new babies could be left in their prams outside. Aunt Alice also had a new addition to her family. My cousin Marie was born in July 1939. My mother not only was shocked at seeing Meyer dead; she believed that if a person committed suicide, their spirit would walk around. She was afraid to live in our house on Tasker Street. I was almost five years of age. It made me wonder. I thought if Meyer never came to visit us in the first place and he died in his own house then why would he want to be walking around our house?

God closes one door and opens another. I did not only hear that from Aunt Mary, but from almost everyone in the neighborhood. My mother also said it but in a different way. She told us if we have faith, it would all work out. All will work out in the end for the greater honor and glory of God. She told us that we should never give up no matter what happens. I thought if God is working all the time for us then why she is scared to live in our house. I just thought it but I did not say it.

In September of 1939, Hitler, the former house painter and wallpaper hanger had the German troops storm into Poland. Stuka dive-bombers had poured over the Polish Frontier and converged on Warsaw. It was called the Blitz. My friend, Anna was half polish on her mother's side. She could not understand everything; however, she told me it was bad. Polish people may have no way of getting out of Poland. Some were able to escape. Polish people started to integrate throughout our neighborhood. Dining room sets were sent to basements, in order to provide sleeping quarters for their Polish relatives that were fortunate enough to get out. Sometimes, the people were not even related to the Polish displaced people. Good, kind people made room for the Polish.

In November of 1939, I started to hear words like building and loan. They were not coming from the Philco radio this time. It seems Aunt Mary and Uncle Sam's building loan went up. I did not know what it meant but I did gather that Aunt Mary and Uncle Sam were in financial difficulty. Daddy still owned the house on Mountain Street. They decided that we would take over Aunt Mary and Uncle Sam's large house on Front Street where all the family wakes were hosted. Aunt Mary and Uncle Sam would move to daddy's house on Mountain Street. Daddy signed the house over to them. Aunt Mary was prim and proper Lace Curtains Irish. The great big skeleton was that Aunt Mary and Uncle Sam had to go on relief or welfare; that was until Uncle Sam died Thanksgiving week, in 1940. Friends in our neighborhood invited me to Thanksgiving dinner. I ate three dinners in all. I received nickels from people. Aunt Mary and Uncle Sam collected six hundred dollars total during the years they were on relief or welfare. Aunt Mary paid them back every penny. In the interim Uncle Sam died and he was the first corpse in our new house. Now all was secure. It would not be advertised that they were on welfare. It was not as if the bad pay wagon would come around and sit in front of a person's door advertising, "these people are on welfare." Aunt Mary said the bad pay wagon sat in front of so many houses in our neighborhood that nobody cared. Besides, the guys that drove the bad pay wagons had no interest in the particular company that was advertising the people were bad pay. Sometimes, they could not find a parking spot in front of the bad pay person's house. They would then sit in front of a good pay person's house. The good pay people did not mind having the bad pay wagon sit outside of their house. People looked out for each other, with the uncertainty of whether they would be visited by the bad pay wagon sometime in the future. Because times were tough for everyone in our neighborhood, it did not matter where the bad pay wagon sat.

Now, prim and proper Aunt Mary would never have the bad pay wagon personally, because she was on welfare and paid her utility bills and taxes in a timely manner. She had enough elegant clothes to last her a lifetime if need be. Her furniture was as elegant. Of course, she had too much furniture, but her pieces were priceless. A cherry wood desk stood in the corner of her tiny living room. There was a Grandfather's Clock that looked as if it came right out of a Williamsburg, Virginia mansion. She was meticulous and if she wanted to do all that dusting, it was nobody's business but her own. She thought being on welfare also was nobody's business, so nobody told us. However, the skeleton came marching out one Thursday afternoon. Bobby went skipping up Mountain Street singing, "hooray, hooray, today's apple day." See how things work out. The only thing we did not like about the move to Front Street was that we would not get Atmore's apples anymore. We could not cross little Fernon Street by ourselves. However, every time it rains, it rains pennies from heaven. Aunt Mary and Uncle Sam were now on relief and the apples came along with it. However, so did the advertisement. Now mind you, nobody cared but Aunt Mary. The apple wagon stopped at almost every house in the neighborhood. Bobby sure was happy.

CHAPTER 8

Philadelphia's police cars are now blue and white. They were once all red. Mayor Rizzo changed that in the 1970s. Aunt Mary called the police cars the Red Devils. She called the padded wagon the big Red Dragon. The Red Devil and the Red Dragons did a booming business in our neighborhood on weekends and holidays. Holy days were more subdued, except for Saint Patrick's Day. Then there were reinforcements for the Red Devils and the Red Dragons. One Saint Paddy's day a man of English descent was celebrating so much that the Red Devils had to be summoned. He was a big man who would not go. They called the Red Dragon for reinforcement. After fighting and fighting with the cops, he conceded, he would go. Wait a minute! He would not go that willingly. He told them he would go if they would let him bring his five-pound corned beef with him, they conceded. Therefore, off they went with Mr. Beefeater and his five-pound corned beef. He was singing about anything that came into his inebriated brain. He told them that he did not like this guy, Hitler and that he was going to do something about it. He then went on to sing, "If you don't like your Uncle Sammy, go back to your land across the sea." People were not so political correct then and remarks could be made about various denominations without anyone taking umbrage. There was no malice. They were part of our melting pot family. He said Hitler would not get Jew Margaret or her family. He would protect them. That is what she was called. She was a very pleasant heavyset woman, who was Jew Gert's mother. The police did not mind his ramblings until he started on the Wops; <Machtu>

bad, we knew that was not right. We would never say that. The one Italian cop became very upset and fed up with Mr. Beefeater. The other cop in the Red Devil calmed him down. He told him there is no tax on talk. The other cop was an Irishman. It sounded like something Aunt Mary would say. The Polish neighbors called us the Irishers. We called the Polish, the Polocks. The name is listed as Polacks in some dictionaries. We had some interracial families in our neighborhood. The three families that I knew just preferred to be white. Their heritage was evident. My friend Mulatto's mother was a big woman whose great grandfather was black. She looked more black than white. Her siblings looked more white than black. There were the black sections where they kept to themselves for the most part. Many lived in the courts speckled in the South Philly area. I remember how they dressed for Sunday church services. They wore big hats and fancy dresses. The spirituality emitted from their souls. I always longed to go where they went on Sunday mornings. However, in those days Catholics were not permitted to go into another denominational church. There was one court off Bainbridge Street where the poor Blacks and the poor Irish lived among each other. They were not a community. The children did not know that and played together from morning until evening in the summertime. There were games that were made up. Nobody had money for games from the 5&10 store called Woolworth. Occasionally someone would get a bag of marbles or a ball and jack set from Woolworth. They cost five cents each. The marbles were used for all types of games. Shoot the marble always reminded me of the South Philly version of pool, without the stick, of course. Whoever shot the marble into the hole, made especially for that game, won. Then there was Stick Ball, Mother may I? Red Rover, Truth or Consequences. We guessed movie stars names from initials. The first question was always, male or female.

There was one game that was called, Find the Liar. Someone put the name of a movie out there. At least one person from each team had seen the movie. I was going strong one day convincing them that I had seen the movie. Reds Lafferty asked me about the big bridge that had fallen down in the movie. "Yes, that scared me." Reds grinned and said, "Aha, got ya! You didn't see it because there was no bridge in the movie." I took it on the cuff and went back to playing with my dolls for a few days. Anna Anderson stopped by with her doll baby in a stroller. We took the doll babies for a walk on those hot summer days. I would get over my embarrassment of being caught and in a few days, I would be right back playing Find the Liar. I was hoping that Snow White and the Seven Dwarfs or The Wizard of Oz became the topic. I knew all about those two movies. I did not analyze why Snow White was living with those seven little men. That is how it was then, people did not analyze. Moreover, how in the world could she have put up with all those different personalities of the seven little guys? It did not sound like a fairy tale story to me. It sounded like a fairy tale, period; a nightmare fairy tale. I think I would have preferred to take my chances with the animals. However, one never knows how it will work out when they are running from the animals.

Little Black Sambo was running from the tigers. They eventually tricked themselves and chased each other's tales. They churned a pile of ghi (butter). When Sambo got home, he ate 169 pancakes with butter on top.

Little Boy Blue was sleeping on the job. The sheep were left to fend for themselves.

CHAPTER 9

The summer of 1940 was good for most children in our neighborhood. We played the usual games. If it were an extremely hot evening, entire families would sleep outside sometimes. It was a safe time in America. My main concern was how I would be able to go under the water spewing out of the fire hydrant. I remembered that fire hydrant was why my mother moved to Fernon Street. Therefore, I did not even bother to ask her for permission. If I did not ask, she could not say no, than I would not be guilty of disobeying my mother. The problem now was Aunt Mary. The fire hydrant was turned on around two p.m. Aunt Mary was usually sitting outside in her beach chair. I consulted with my friends and we came up with a great idea. I was small. <Tschutti> a friend suggested that we get a discarded tire from the vacant lot. I could go inside of it. They could then wheel me right past Aunt Mary. They will say, "Hello, Aunt Mary." Everyone called my Aunt Mary, "Aunt Mary." Really, she was my Aunt Mary, my father's sister. Okay, good plan. They wheeled me past Aunt Mary and she replied, "Hello hon," to the first one that said hello. I was not found out. Hooray, I was having so much fun, I stayed in the tire and it became a new sport game in our neighborhood called Tire Splash.

I do not even know if Aunt Mary would have objected to me going under the plug, as the fire hydrant was called in our neighborhood. I did not want to take a chance. Aunt Mary had some airs about her that my mother did not have. My mother had some airs about her that Aunt Mary did not have. I knew from my mother and father's move to Fernon Street that going under the fire hydrant would not be allowed by my mother. Now mind you, I never asked her the question, May I? Therefore, I was not guilty of disobeying my mother. I was certain the answer would be no.

Maggie Twisty Stockings told Aunt Mary that she thought the kids were up to something with that discarded tire. Aunt Mary related the story to me. She added, "She is a P. I." I laughed and laughed. I never in a million years would think such a thing would come out of Aunt Mary's mouth. I conjured up visions of a P. I. I thought it was obscene. Years later that I learned that she meant Private Investigator. She added that she thought the cigars Maggie Twisty Stockings smoked were affecting her brain. That cleared up for me why Maggie always smelled. I thought it was B.O. (body odor.) Then I knew it was cigar odor.

My father took me to the HI HO SILVER bar on Oregon Avenue. It was a very hot, humid Saturday afternoon in June of 1940. He needed to meet Dominic there. Dominic worked as a bartender on Saturday afternoons. Dominic was part of the crew that daddy supervised for the City of Philadelphia. Daddy showed Dominic the new City car that had been assigned to daddy. After Dominic inspected the car, we went inside the bar. Both daddy and I had soda.

It was on the house. I noticed the cash register. I liked the sound it made, Cachinga! Money was going into the cash register so fast. I watched every movement while I drank my Frank's orange soda, which was made in South Philly.

When we returned home, I told Bobby all about it. I told him I could start a business if he would be the customer. He agreed. I said we would wait until Wednesday when mom will be upstairs doing her wash.

On Wednesday, I set up my little pink table and chair set that my Uncle Doc had given to me. I put my cigar box on my little pink buffet that came with the dining room set. I cut dollar size bills from the newspaper. I then took my mother's bingo chips to use as change. I told Bobby we were all set but we needed another customer. I went over to the next-door house and asked if Dotsie could come over to our house to play as we were opening a new business and needed another customer. Dotsie's grandmother spoke Polish, with enough English in between that a non-Polish person could understand what she was saying. She told Dotsie's mother to let Dotsie go over to our house. They are good people. The daddy goes to work everyday. The mother cooks dinner every day. The mother hangs out the whitest sheets in the neighborhood. The daddy does not drink, like some of the Irishers in the neighborhood. The Aunt Mary stretches her Easter curtains on the wooden curtain stretcher that she owns. Let Dotsie go over to their house. While she was doing a good biography on our family, she never did ask what type of business we were opening. Since she asked me no questions, I told her no lies.

I coached Bobby how to act. I told him to order a drink and then buy one for Dotsie. I told him to order another and then order one for the house including the bartender. He was one month away from turning four years of age, but caught on fast. I then went and retrieved the gallon of Dago Red wine from behind the cellar door. Since nobody in our house drank, it just sat there since Christmas time. That was when Dominic and Angelo brought it with figs, nuts, fruit and cheese. They brought every delicacy imaginable for a Christmas feast of treats.

We started the business. Bobby said, "I'll have one, give Dotsie one on me." Dotsie said, "Huh, what kind of business are we playing?" Bobby drank his. Dotsie drank some of her drink. She said "I feel funny, I'm going home." She staggered through the dining room and living room. Grampy Brennan was sitting by the window in the living room. He had his cap pulled down over his eyes. As long as there was no commotion, he assumed we were playing nice. Bobby ordered another and bought me one. Cachinga! I had almost five dollars in fake money in my cigar box. In a short while, we weaned down. I went to the living room and went to sleep in front of the fireplace. Bobby went around the corner to Aunt Mary's house. He kept running around her dining room table. Aunt Mary opened her front door. She saw BoBo, the midget. She asked him if he would go quickly and summon Boy's father. She added that something was wrong with Boy. BoBo ran as fast as he could. Aunt Mary yelled, "Hurry BoBo." He said, "I am hurrying, Aunt Mary." By the time BoBo reached our house, he was out of breath from running. He knocked on our door. My father went to the door. He looked out the window on the door. He mumbled to himself, "I swear that I heard someone knocking on the front door." He turned to go back into the living room. The knocking continued. This time he opened the door. BoBo was standing there. He was exhausted and sweating from running from Aunt Mary's house to our house. BoBo finally got the words out. "Aunt Mary said you must hurry, something is wrong with Boy." He then pondered and said, "I guess she means Bobby." Daddy thanked him and told him that he was a good boy. Daddy had observed me sleeping in front of the fireplace, which was not unusual. I did that often on a hot summer afternoon. He decided to go out the back door because it was closer to Aunt Mary's house. He passed the remnants of my bar business. He then knew what was wrong with Boy. He carried Bobby home and put him into bed. Bobby slept for twenty-four hours. They just let me sleep until I woke up which was around the same time Bobby had awakened. We then were questioned. My father kept looking at the cat-o-nine tails hanging on the wall going into the closet to the cellar. He did not use it. He never used it. It just was hanging there to intimidate us and it did. When the story came out, my father said, "I'll be go to hell." Mother said, "Do you know your ancestors were the Rittenhouses and Brennans-on-the-Moor?" Of course, I knew when to quit when I was ahead. I would have liked to tell her that I have the genes of the first director of the United States Mint, David Rittenhouse. Cachinga!

$$\$\$\$ \; \boxed{=} \; \$\$\$$$

As summer was ebbing into fall and the prospect of going to school loomed over me, I had a desire to start another business. This time I was going to use real money. The FDIC was now in place. I did not know what I would sell until the idea came. One hot summer day I was walking up Mountain Street to Aunt Mary's house. My sister Marie and Dotsie's brother Sonny were on the south side of Mountain Street selling lemonade. They had a makeshift stand. It consisted of a wooden box with wire around it. It held produce that had been delivered to Mrs. White's store at Front and Fernon Streets. She said they could have it for their business. I thought since I had the yearning to start another business and they were already in business, I would ask if I could participate. Sonny was willing, but Marie said, "Get lost twerp." That hurt my feelings. I was not going to let it hurt my financial status as well. I asked Andy Piernock if he would watch my furniture as I brought out the needed pieces. He said he would. I brought out the little pink table and a chair for me to sit. I still did not have a product to sell. I went into the kitchen. My mother had a humongous pot of bean soup cooking on the stove. It was hot and I knew it. I also knew that I did not want to impose on Mrs. Gilbert again, to heal me from another burn, God knows where this time. Therefore, I dumped cold water into the soup and mixed it good. The soup was so thick before the water was added that it could have been used for bean stew. Another problem that I encountered was that it was heavy. I knocked on Francis Egger's door and asked him if he would help me carry it from the kitchen to the table on Mountain Street. He was older than I was. He said he would. He did not ask me any questions, so I did not have to tell him any lies. I then asked Andy Piernock if he would continue to keep watch over my business until I got the ladle. He complied. I was in business. I did not know how much to charge for the soup. I had never sold soup before. I did not use real money in my first business. So, May Kane comes by the stand and asks Andy Piernock if he will go into the back gate of Corky Purvi's house and put five cents on 245. Aha! I have it. I will charge two ladles for five cents. Of course, they needed to bring their own container. Dealing with nickels was a cinch for me. I knew there were twenty nickels in a dollar. I never was mean and I did not intend to put Marie and Sonny out of business, it just evolved that way. I sold the entire pot of soup within a half hour. They could not cheat me with the containers they brought with them, because it was two ladles full for five cents. It did not matter if they greased the containers or not. It would not affect the amount of soup that they bought. People in our neighborhood greased the pitcher when they were chasing the duck. That way the pitcher of beer would not be all suds and no beer or just a little beer. When they went to the saloon with their own pitcher to be filled with beer, it was called chasing the duck. I was already out of the bar business and I had no concerns if they wanted to grease the container for the bean soup. Ah, life was good. I made two one-dollar bills, four quarters, two dimes and four nickels. Moreover, to boot, the FDIC was in effect. I bet it would not be long before I could fill my cigar box and take it to the bank. Of course, my father would need to go with me. I wanted to stay away from Savings and Loan companies. I did not know if the FDIC backed them, but I did not like what they did to Aunt Mary and Uncle Sam. It was the principle of the thing. Everything was working out for me for my bean soup business. Just because I had to go out of business one time and stop drinking for quite a long time, it did not mean that I could never operate another business successfully. As luck had it, my mother was taking a bath when I brought the bean soup out of the kitchen. Marie ran around and opened our front door. She was yelling, "She's selling our supper." Mom answered, "SOUP." She could not hear clearly, because the door to the bathroom was closed. Marie persisted, "She's selling our soup." My mother answered, "BEAN." I sold the entire pot before my mother went to the kitchen to add water to the thick soup and put it on low to cook until suppertime. Lo and behold! There was no soup. She mused to herself; I have never displaced a pot of soup before this. The story came to light. Marie made sure of that. My mother called for me to come into the house. This time I needed to summon Chuckie Geiger to watch my stand with the empty soup pot and ladle. I went into the house through the alley. My mother said, "Do you know anything about the pot of soup that is missing?" I said "Yes." She said, "What?" I had my cigar box with me. Now I had to face my mother. I had not thought that out. I kept learning the pitfalls of each business as I went along. I fail and get up again. However, I will learn eventually how to be more business savvy. What can I say? When the story unraveled, she was in shock. She did not say, "I'll be go to hell," like daddy said when he discovered the remnants of my first business. She said, "Glory be. What on earth processed you to sell our supper?" I looked at her with my big blue innocent eyes and said, "I didn't know I was doing anything wrong." I never want the building and loan to go up on us and necessitate a move. I held the cigar box up and said, "I was only trying to help the family out by having money for a rainy day." I had heard Aunt Mary say we need to put some money away for a rainy day. She glared down at me. This was serious as she did not say wait until your father comes home. She was angry. The ominous looking cat-o-nine tails was hanging right there by the cellar door. I copped a plea, just as one of the gangsters did in a movie. I said, "You don't want God to take me back to heaven, like he did the little angel who was eating too many of Mrs. Parker's mincemeat cookies, do you?" She did not hesitate. She said, "No, No, Never." I said I am only a little kid and I just did not understand. I will not reach the age of reason for four more months. She replied, "Okay, go out and bring your stuff into the house." She went on to say, "Maybe it's too hot for soup today anyway." She said that we would have ground meat and gravy instead. We had ground meat and gravy about three times a week. We bought the ground meat at Jules butcher shop on the 1800 block of south Second Street. The butcher shop was painted green on the outside. It had a great big storefront window. Inside atop the wooden floor was sawdust. We went almost every day because we did not have freezers yet. We were lucky that we had a "Frigidaire" refrigerator. The meat lasted for another meal also. We were able to use the ice cube compartment to freeze the meat. My father was paid by dates, the first and the fifteenth of each month. It did not matter how many days were in the month. If it was a long month, the food had to be stretched. We did not know it. After mother doctored it up, we thought it was the same as usual. Marie was called to supper. She looked at it and whined, "Are we having this slop again?"

The usual lecture followed from my father. "Do you know how many starving people there are in this world?" Do you know there are dictators who keep people from shopping for food?" Do you know dogs eat better in America than some people in other countries?" At that moment, I wished I knew how to get to those countries. I would have sacrificed my dinner for that evening. Not because I thought it was slop, but because I felt like crying for the starving people. One consolation that I had was that there would not be any starving people in our neighborhood that particular night. I already had provided most of the families with bean soup. I took one of my nickels the following Sunday and put it in the poor box at Sacred Heart Church. It was my little way of doing something about it. Maybe if everybody in the world gave one nickel, people would not be starving.

Not many families had the conveniences that we had, including a mangle iron much like the Chinese used to iron shirtsleeves and anything else that would be less work for them. However, I do not think that was on the Chinese minds those days as much as Japan seizing Manchuria, part of Northeastern China. By taking over Manchuria, Japan gained rich supplies of coal and iron. Japan created a state called Manchukuo in the area. Despite Aunt Mary's warning about the Chinese on Second Street in South Philly, I knew that was not right what the dictators were doing to them. China called on the League of Nations to help. The League condemned Japanese aggression but did little else. The United States refused to recognize Manchukuo but took no other action against Japan.

The tea was brewing in China towns all over America. Something horrible was brewing for their country. The mad dictators did not care about anything but power and wealth. I just knew it was not fair. However, I was not six years of age yet and I did not know the world was not fair. That is why I needed to trust God. My mother told me that God brings good out of bad. In my own little private world, I was out of business. Of course, I received a nickel here and there for summoning someone to Convey's candy store to answer a telephone call. Not too many people in our neighborhood had telephones. When a kid summoned someone to the phone at the corner store, a nickel was given. It was standard procedure. In addition, the number winners continued to tip me if they thought my prayers brought the winning numbers that day. I collected money when my mother was cleaning out the closets. Oh, it was not on a grand scale. She did have some clothes that were passed down so many times that it was time for Sid Waterside to get them.

CHAPTER 10

Sid owned the rag shop. He collected rags, copper and anything that he could resell for a profit. Sid Waterside was a cheat. He held his finger on the scale so it would come up to a lower number. Cheat us once that's on you; cheat us twice that's on us. After the word circulated, the kids in our neighborhood took bundles and bundles of papers to Sid. What Sid did not know was that the inside of the papers were saturated with water. The entire salvaged items that were collected and taken to him were doctored up so it would come out even.

Shortly before I started school, I opened another business. It came about unexpectedly. Aunt Mary went food shopping on Friday evenings. She went to The Big Bear Supermarket in West Philadelphia. My parents took her. She did not want to leave Uncle Sam alone for any length of time. He was sick. I would turn six in less than four months at the time. She told me that if I sat with Uncle Sam, she would buy me a one-pound box of chocolate candy. Cachinga! I agreed to do the job on Friday evenings. It enabled me to establish another business of my own. I told Uncle Sam funny stories. I made him laugh. I thought that his personality was getting better. Then, Bobby came in carrying Aunt Mary's groceries. Uncle Sam uttered "grr." I told him, "You knock that off, Cuckoo." He did.

I never did find out what was wrong with Uncle Sam that I had to stay with him. It was something serious, though, because the following November, he died. That is how he became the first corpse in our house since we took over the ownership of the house, where the wakes were held.

Since it was summertime, I kept the chocolate candy in the refrigerator. I put a blouse over it. Thus if anyone else went into the refrigerator, they would not want to eat it. Mother often sprinkled her clothes and placed them in the refrigerator for a short while. It made it easier for her to iron them. I would never deprive anyone of taking anything they wanted to eat out of the refrigerator. I was always like that; I would not do that. I was not exactly hiding my candy; I would not do that either. I had to take my chances if anyone discovered it. That was okay. When supper was over every evening and I was dressed in my sundress that I wore after my bath every afternoon, I took my candy and cigar box and sat on the front step. I opened my business from five p.m. to five thirty p.m. I could not keep the chocolates outside for too long, they would melt. In that half hour, I did a booming business. I caught people before they arrived at the corner candy store that was two doors away from our house. Competition was tough. I needed to have a strategy. Cachinga! I will advertise imported chocolate candy. The imported part was that they came from West Philadelphia into our little neighborhood of South Philly. Not one person ever asked from where they were imported. It sounded so good. Sometimes, I sold out immediately on a Saturday evening. The price was one cent each not two for one cent, but one cent each. They were imported. Cachinga!

"Joan at Philadelphia waterfront, waiting for her imported chocolates"-

CHAPTER 11

Towards the end of August, my mother took me to John Wanamaker Department Store. To go to the grand scale Wanamaker Store was an adventure in itself. It was regal and glamorous. Rich people shopped there. It had a huge sculptured bronze eagle that looked over the great marble balcony. Beneath the great eagle was the organ that provided the music at scheduled times throughout the day. That was the pivotal place to meet friends and relatives, under the eagle. At Christmastime, the children would sit on the floor in awe as the sugar fairies danced animatedly on the large black curtain. The colors were purple, white, gold, green and red, lots of red. The Nutcracker by Tschkofski played. The floor where I sat was in the perfume section. The sounds, sights and smells made me feel like I was drifting into the heavens. I needed to touch the fabric on the sleeve of my coat between the thumb and index finger of my right hand to feel that I was still here on earth. I longed for a taste of the plum. That was no problem. When the show was over, we went to the Crystal Room, which was the elegant dining room at the Wanamaker store. The society women ate finger sandwiches. My mother permitted me to order any type of food that I chose. I chose not to eat like those society women. I soon forgot about my desire for a plum and ordered a hot roast beef sandwich. I ordered a glass of milk to go with my sandwich. My mother did not want the finger sandwiches either. The Crystal Room was not expensive like some of the fine restaurants in the grand hotels of Philadelphia. The Crystal Room at The Wanamaker Store was as elegant as the dining rooms of the ritzy hotels. However, at Wanamakers the rich and famous and the ordinary citizen could sit in the same dining room and enjoy the fine food of the Crystal Room. Everybody wore hats in those days in the 1940s. My mother bought our clothes at Wanamakers a great deal of the time. We were not wealthy; my mother was an astute shopper. She looked for the sales. She also was very well informed as to the timing and pricing of the various items of clothing. My mother prided herself on the fact that her first job after graduating Commercial School at Sacred Heart of Jesus was as a bookkeeper at John Wanamaker, the most elegant of elegance. She obtained a charge plate when she worked there. She would proudly pull out the Wanamaker charge card from her purse and tell the salesperson how she obtained it and how long it has been serving our family. She was also proud of her achievement of never missing a payment when the charge bill was sent. She used it until they closed their doors forever in the early twenty-first century. I still think of the Wanamaker store at Christmastime and at Easter time. I am so grateful that I had the exposure to Wanamakers. My children also were able to experience Wanamakers. We often came home with our special treasures purchased with my mother's special card, which was light blue. It had her name engraved on the front of the card. It was engraved on an addressograph machine. After lunch in the Crystal Room restaurant, we went to the department for children. They were having a gigantic sale. I was able to pick out my own dress. I selected a tartan plaid dress of red and green with black going through it. It had a round collar trimmed with white lace. It was beautiful. I tried it on. It was a perfect fit. I always felt like a princess when I received new clothing. I always received new clothing for the first day of school and for Christmas and Easter. Sometimes my brand new outfit was a hand me down from Marie. One time, Mrs. Walker, our next-door neighbor brought a coat from her niece, Lorraine Bartels, for me to try on and to wear on Christmas day. It was a perfect fit. It was okay with me. I felt great in it. My mother let me pick out a nice velvet tam hat with a feather. I felt as proud as punch when I was selected to take up the children's collection that Christmas morning. The coat had a velvet purple collar. It had purple leggings that went with it. My mother would try to get Marie to wear hand me downs from my cousin, Sissy Mary Annabelle Lou girl but Marie balked. Marie said, "No way." My mother usually gave into her because she was the oldest and by all appearances, the most dignified. That is by all appearances. One day Marie said, "Come here little twerp. Do you know why Sissy Mary Annabelle Lou girl was born with a punctured ear drum?" I said, "God made her that way?" She told me that God didn't make her that way, that's where the coat hanger got stuck." I did not know what she meant. I asked my mother what a coat hanger had to do with Sissy Mary Annabelle Lou girl's ear. She said "WHAT?" "Where did you hear that?" I told her Marie had told me. It seems Marie was eavesdropping on some conversations on the back streets of our neighborhood. The women talked of swallowing castor oil, iodine and other things that Marie could not remember. If that did not work, they went on to discuss, try a coat hanger. She asked me if I knew where Marie was. I said, "Yes." She said, "Well, where is she?" In our neighborhood, people did not like stool pigeons and I never wanted to have that title. I might wake up dead. My mother asked me a question and I could not tell her a lie. I said Marie went to swimmies. Swimmies was the public swimming pool right next to Sacred Heart School. She said she is not supposed to be at swimmies, there is something going around in our neighborhood called ringworms. I do not want any of you walking around with the Jensen's Violet salve on your skin. Everybody would see it and know that it came from dirt. Oh, that was the four letter word we were not even to think about in our house. This was one of the few times I ever heard my mother mention her heritage. "Do you know I am a descendent of the Rittenhouses? Do you know Grampy is from Brennan on the Moor?"

While mother was citing her heritage, German planes were pounding London and other English cities during the Battle of Britain. British fighter pilots used radar, a new invention to detect the approach of enemy planes. They then took to the air, shooting down thousands of German planes. The British Prime Minister, Winston Churchill warned the people to prepare for an attack. He was courageous. He said even though we could offer only blood, sweat and tears we shall never surrender. He smoked a large cigar and lived at #10 Downing Street in London, England. I remember him. I also was able to interview people from coast to coast who were involved in the bombings. Maureen Fergenson told me she had to run to shelter. Her mother had gone to the bathroom and Maureen could not find her. She envisioned the worse. She said it was horrific to think that her mother lay helpless or dead under the remnants of the German planes that had been shot out of the sky during The Battle of Britain. She expressed the indescribable joy when her mother emerged safe and sound.

It was almost impossible to visualize that Maureen had been through that. She was such a nice British woman who was well read. Everyone I met on the Amtrak cross-country trip had a story for me. I was not only researching, I was having fun. I was meeting people and they were telling me stories eagerly.

"No stories, young lady," mother said to Marie. What were you doing at swimmies?" I think she tackled the easiest situation first. Marie said, "Oh, gee, mother, I thought the ringworm infection was over." Mother said, "Marie, as long as there is dirt to play in on the vacant lots in our neighborhood, the ringworm threat will always be there." Marie thought fast, little did she know what the next confrontation would be. She said, "Oh, mother, swimmies is all cement." That is all that my mother wanted to discuss on that subject. She told Marie not to go to swimmies again until she obtained Mother's permission. Marie told Mother that she would not go again until she receives permission. Now, the biggie; I did not want to miss it, so I postponed making my Jersey (New Jersey) tomato sandwich with mayonnaise until I heard this one. "Marie, where did you ever hear about a coat hanger?" Marie thought fast. She replied, "The street vendor was selling them." "Marie, that's not what I meant. Where did you hear about the castor oil and the coat hangers?" Marie said, "Did I do something wrong, mother?" "Well, let me hear it and I'll tell you if you did something wrong." I usually did not like the possibility of someone getting into trouble, but this one was too good to pass up. My stomach was growling but I had to stay on the stair steps until I heard the explanation. Marie told my mother that Sissy Mary Annabelle Lou girl had told her she had the hole in her eardrum so God would not mix her up with another Sissy Mary Annabelle Lou girl. Mother blurted out,

"Glory be, where in the world could you find another Sissy Mary Annabelle Lou girl? I don't think God had to be concerned about that." {Come on, Marie, tell the truth and shame the devil.} That was one of Aunt Mary's sayings. Marie said, "Well, I was waiting to go to confession last Saturday and while three ladies were standing in line; they were talking. That's where I heard iodine, castor oil and coat hanger." "Good lord, child do you mean they were all confessing the same sin?" Mother answered, "I suppose, strange, isn't it?" {Go on Marie, you know more than your prayers.} She said, "Okay this is the last part; she said the women said the coat hanger was the last resort. If a baby was already present, it could catch on an arm, leg, eye or hand. Mother said, "Okay, I understand." She could not bar Marie from going to confession. She told her to go to confession in the line for children. Mother bought it, but I did not. I knew she was eavesdropping on the women's conversations from one of the back streets. Marie was off the hook.

CHAPTER 12

The prospects of going to school for the first time scared me. I was only five years of age. I was not going to turn six for three more months. I was a baby. Most of my classmates had already turned six. I voiced my apprehension. I was cool about it, because my image was always important to me. I did not want anyone calling me fraidy cat or chanting, "Baby, baby, stick your head in gravy."

My father's cousin, Arthur, and his wife, Elizabeth, were "on." That is how my family described visitors who were from far away, or even if they were from one state away. Arthur and Elizabeth lived in California. These relatives were going to stop in New England to see more of the family. They were going to be "off" around noon on that beautiful September day.

Elizabeth came into my room to hug me and kiss me before I left for school. She said really nice things about me. Before I knew it, tears started streaming down my face. She asked, "What's the matter, baby?" I did not take her calling me baby as an insult. It made me feel so special. I told her, "I'm too scared to go to school." The great brick building reminded me of a prison. It even has an iron fence around it. That was the perspective from a five year old child. Sacred Heart actually is a small school and it is a warm school. The statue of The Sacred Heart of Jesus stands in front of the main entrance. The essence of spirituality prevails. Elizabeth thought she would help me with the first step of facing going to school. She said, "Baby, you go to school this morning. When you come home for lunch, we will take you to New England with us." I said "Okay,

I will, I can do that." Wow! Good deal. I would only have to go to school for three and one half-hours. My father drove my sister, Marie and me to school. His 1940 Ford pulled up in front of Sacred Heart School. He kissed each of us on the cheek. He said your guardian angels are with you. What he did not know was that my guardian angel and I was going to be "off" right after lunch.

Sister Mary Edna assigned me to a desk in the first row. It was a single desk. I was about the fifth student in the aisle of desks. A name card had my name written on it. It was covered in plastic. It was about eight inches long by three inches high. It was covered with plastic so I could see my name and not smudge it and then maybe change it to Moriso or something other than my true name. It may even change my nationality. It was the most beautiful handwriting I had ever seen. It also was a teaching tool so I could learn to write my name. Today, I am told that I have beautiful handwriting. I aspired to learn to write my name like it was on the card that was covered with plastic. It crossed my mind to take it home with me because I was going to be "off" to New England; however, Sister Mary Edna told us what to take home with us at lunchtime. There was no mention of the name card, so I just knew I should not take it home. I would have to find another way to learn to write my name like that. Now it put me into the yin and yang mode. Part of me wanted to stay until I learned to write my name like that. I already knew my numbers. I also knew all of my prayers. After thinking it over once again, I decided that I would go to New England and learn to write my name like that some other time.

The introduction to first grade was cut short because a boy named Donald had a seizure. He sat in the very last aisle in the front desk; that is, until he fell out of it. Sister Edna immediately ran to his assistance. She knew what to do until the paramedics came. She sent the brownie in the first seat in the first aisle to tell Mother Cyrilla to call for help. Oh, she was not a formal member of the Brownie troop, which evolved in third grade. Every class has one or two brownies. It seemed as if the nuns had radar, as they always picked a brownie for the first desk in the first aisle. The brownie seems to have been coached on how to answer a door properly. She would never yell, "Come in." She would never open the door and say, "What do you want?" She was always prim and proper and said, "Good morning Sister, or good morning, Father." When the priest came into our classroom, we always had to stand up and say in unison "Good morning Father" or if it were afternoon, we would say in unison, "Good afternoon Father." The brownie always had her lines down pat. She never wavered. She must have been coached on how to be a brownie since the days she could walk or talk. When the brownie went to the principal's office that day, Mother Cyrilla knew something must have happened to one of the babies. That was the mantra, "First grade babies." Mother Cyrilla listened when the brownie told her what had happened. The brownie would never volunteer to say more than Sister Edna told her to say; however, when Mother Cyrilla asked her, she did not hesitate. She described the happenings. Mother Cyrilla did not hesitate. She immediately called the paramedics. Sister Mary Edna sprang into action while the brownie was going for further assistance. She put a stick on Donald's tongue. We sat silently and prayed. I rather knew Donald would be okay. I had known children in our neighborhood who had suffered from seizures; they always bounced back. Never once did I think Sister Mary Edna was being sadistic by putting a popsicle like stick on his tongue. Instead of the popsicle, it had gauze. I thought Sister Mary Edna already had eaten the popsicle and then wrapped the stick in gauze. That was not accurate as I was only five years of age and did not reach the age of reason yet. Part of the thinking stemmed from my observation that Sister Mary Edna was five feet tall and five feet wide.

Shortly after Donald went home, school was dismissed for the morning session. I was looking forward to going to New England; however, the best made plans of mice and men often go astray. Daddy picked us up for lunch break. He had his City car because he took his lunch break to bring us home from school and to take us back to school for the afternoon. I thought it best not to mention that I would not need the chauffeur services for the afternoon session. We arrived home. Mother had our hot dittalinis ready. She had the small pasta covered with cheese and tomato sauce. We had that about three times a week. Even though it looked and smelled delicious, I immediately ran upstairs. Mother thought I was going to the bathroom; however, I was going to get my suitcase. Then it dawned on me. I had not seen Elizabeth. I came downstairs and asked where Elizabeth was. Daddy said, "Well of course she is "off." They are going to be "on" in Rhode Island in two days." They are taking their time and seeing some sights they don't see on the West coast." Oy vey, West coast, East coast, Rhode Island and trickery.

Bag and baggage, they were off. I was shocked and had trusted Elizabeth. She made a deal with me and I expected her to keep her end of the bargain. I had kept mine. I went to school for the morning. I did not curse or anything, I just put it into my mind's book of experiences for the time being. My yin and yang were so confused. I started to remember the name card. That was an enticement to go back to school for the afternoon session. {No! Not enough, I have been had. Oh, how cheap.} That is what people in our neighborhood said when they were had. I tried and tried to reason it out; however, the result was, I have been had. I still tried to keep cool. I told the family; Elizabeth told me they were going to take me to New England with them when I came home for lunch. Now, while everyone agreed she should not have done that, and maybe meant no harm, it happened, and I have been had. Bobby came up to me before we left for the afternoon session. He was only four years of age but he tried to reason things out for me. He said, "Why would you want to go to England, anyway, they are bombing over there?" We did not know where over there was. We did not know where Rhode Island in New England was. However, it still did not sit right with me. There is a fly in the ointment. That was one of Aunt Mary's sayings meaning things are not adding up. Our little Philco radio was announcing, because of the war in Europe, Franklin Delano Roosevelt was running for a third term. England is in Europe. Oy vey, I am getting a headache. I heard Mrs. White say that.

Now, I was still bargaining with myself. Maybe it just slipped Elizabeth's mind. I did not buy that. Maybe she could forget a hat or a bottle of shampoo, but forgetting a little kid would be stretching things too much. I bargained all the way to Sacred Heart School for the afternoon session. "No, No," I said to myself, "It is not right. Fair is fair; I am not supposed to be at the afternoon session on my first day of school. I am supposed to be on my way to Rhode Island."

Daddy's 1940 sedan pulled up in front of Sacred Heart School on that beautiful September afternoon. He opened the door for us. Marie was in the front seat. Her friends, Sarah Jane and Teresa were in the back with me. They proceeded to alight from the car. I then had enough room to lie on the floor of the car. Daddy, said, "Come on, you don't want to be late, do you?" I thought no, I do not want to be late. I do not want to be there at all and I immediately silently recited a mantra, "No, no, I won't go, I have been had." Suppose this spread all over the neighborhood. What if the announcer on the Philco radio said FDR is running for a third term and Joan Morrisroe has been had. I would be the laughing stock of the waterfront district. So, no, no, I will not go. Daddy said, "Come on Joan." I stiffened up. I kept my eye on Donald earlier in the day. I stiffened up like that, except I remained conscious and did not convulse. No, no I will not go. Daddy spotted my cousin, Charlie Powers. He was captain of the Safeties. That is what we called the Crossing Patrol or the Safety Patrol. They were the days before crossing guards. I loved Charlie; he was good. He had a speech impediment. Nobody ever messed with him about it, as he was respected in the neighborhood. Besides, we had so many aunts, uncles and cousins; it was just smart not to mess with any of us. Charlie tried to get me to come out. If I would come out for anyone, it would have been Charlie. Mother Cyrilla came out. She was a sweet nun who was principal of Sacred Heart School. She was unassuming and humble. She just listened to God and did her job as best as she could. She loved the children. She could not reason with me. Daddy would not give me a good smack across part of my anatomy right in front of Sacred Heart School for all to see. There was quite a crowd by now. The cop on the beat was summoned. He could not persuade me. No, no, I will not go. I have been had. Daddy said, "Enough." He pulled me out by my feet and the police officer held his long arms out for my tiny body to fit into them. I was out of the car. Daddy carried me into the first grade classroom, which was right next to the humongous statue of The Sacred Heart of Jesus. The Sacred Heart knew that I had been had and that was the reason I was rebelling. He looked out at me as if He still loved me.

OOOOOOOO

Glory Be To The Father:

Glory be to the father
And to the son
And to the Holy Ghost

As it was in the beginning
Is now and ever shall be
World without end.

Amen

Sister Mary Edna instructed daddy to put me in my seat. The name card was still there. As soon as daddy was out of sight, I started crying and wailing. Sister Mary Edna then changed my seat. She put me in the next aisle where the double desks stood. I tried to escape. She put four people in the double desk and that was not counting me. I had guards. Chez! What a day. However, the worse was yet to come. I cried and wailed for over an hour. Sister Mary Edna appeared by the side of the big double desk where I was being guarded. She instructed the guards to go back to their assigned seats. She took me into the cloakroom. I thought, finally, I am getting on her nerves so much, she is going to summon one of my cousins from seventh or eighth grade to take me home. The only concern I had was why the cloakroom. I did not wear a coat. I went into the cloakroom with her. Sister Mary Edna said, "Do you see that round radiator cover?" How could I miss it? It was heavy wrought iron and had a big iron knob on it. Maybe she was going to smuggle me out to save face. I thought it was a tunnel. It turned out to be a cover for the furnace. I answered, "Yes, I see it sister." She then went under the front flap of her habit and brought out the largest pair of scissors I had ever seen. She told me that if I did not stop crying, she would cut my nose off. She would then toss it down there. {Sure.} My parents would not notice that they sent me to school with a nose and I came home without a nose. I could have d-doubled dared her, silently, of course. However, it was almost two p.m. and I was tired. I did not surrender or anything, I just wanted to take my nap. I was only five years of age. She said, "Okay we'll try again." She took me back to the original seat that I had been assigned in the morning. My name card still stood there. I wanted to put my head down and take a nap immediately. First, I had to do something to save face. I forced myself to put a big smile on my face and then I put my head down and went to sleep.

The other kids thought she bought my silence and were wondering what she gave me. Bingo! I saved face. If I had gone home and told my parents about the afternoon session, it would turn out that Sister was right. Sister was always right. Despite their mentality about nuns, I formed my own opinions that Sister was not always right, no, not always. However, I kept that to myself. Daddy pulled up in front of Sacred Heart School at three p.m. He just assumed that everything had worked out. Marie and her friends were gibbering. I went into the house. My mother said how it went. I replied "Ask me no questions, I'll tell you no lies." Then I took off like a bat out of hell to my bedroom. I quoted Edgar Allen Poe, "Nevermore." Only I did not know Edgar Allen Poe had already coined the word. I learned that later. "Nevermore." I needed a strategy. I always sat where I had access to the front door or to the fire escape door. Sometimes it turned out that way because I was small, sometimes because I was very bright. My strategy was that I needed to sit where I could have easy access to either door, if necessary.

First grade actually became enjoyable. I was learning how to write my name, the same as it was on the name card in front of me. I was learning my Aa, Bb, Cc's and numbers. I was learning more numbers than I thought existed. I liked that. We participated in the Forty Hours Procession that took place in Sacred Heart Church. The Forty Hours Procession was held after there had been forty hours of adoration to the Blessed Sacrament. We strewed daisies from a hand held wicker basket. We sang songs to the Blessed Sacrament. We sang them in Latin.

Tantum ergo Sacramentium
Down in adoration falling,
Veneremur cernui,
This great Sacrament we hail;
Et antiquum documentum
Over ancient forms of worship
Novo cedat ritui;
Newer rites of grace prevail;
Praestet fides supplementum,
Faith will tell us Christ is present,
Sensuum defectui.
When our human senses fail.

Saint Thomas Aquinas, 1227-1274

SACRED HEART SCHOOL

CHAPTER 13

Christmastime was especially enjoyable. The room and windows were carefully decorated with images of the Birth of Christ. We also had Poinsettias around. There was a five feet Christmas tree. There was a little image of Santa Claus. The Big Day was all about Christ. I still believed in Santa Claus. I went on believing until Marie told me that Santa Claus was just made up so kids would behave. She also went on to say some other stuff that I did not understand. She said only Captain America and angels could fly. I told her that I did not want to hear her propaganda. Only I did not know words like that then. I did not want her to take Santa Claus away from me. I was just wishing that Santa Claus would hear her. That would teach her. Sister Mary Edna stood inside the cloakroom right before Christmas break that year. She instructed us to line up according to how we were seated. We complied. She said we each are to go into the cloakroom on the right hand side and exit through the left hand side door. Sister Mary Edna gave each child a little box of hard candies. The box could be pulled open to transform into The Nativity scene. That was so kind of her. She then pulled three children out of the line and told them to wait. I was one of them. After the other kids passed through, the three of us stood there. She then handed each of us a small box. That was besides the candy that we had received. Each contained a beautiful gold miraculous medal and chain. I loved it; however, I started to think why there were three of us selected. I went on to think if she was holding out on the other kids, maybe she even was holding out on me. I dismissed that thought immediately.

The reason she selected the three children to stand aside for a bonus gift was that their parents had done favors for her. Personally, I thought if she wanted to repay the parents, she should give the parents the gifts. Oh well, two parents each, times one gift each, would come out to six. This way if she gave it to the child instead of the parents, it would come out to three.

I was so happy that day. I brought my candy home. I did not even get the notion to sell it. It was connected to the Nativity. I put my medal and chain around my neck. Father Cavanaugh had already blessed it. We then proceeded to put on the first grade version of the Christmas pageant.

I was mesmerized that Christmas morning. My doll had been missing for two weeks. I came downstairs on Christmas morning and found my doll with brand new clothing on her stuffed cotton body. Her porcelain face, arms and legs were shining. Her hair was beautiful; it looked like a new head of blond hair. I immediately picked her up. I then saw that she had been sitting on a brown wicker doll chair that was new. I also received a little pink coach if I chose to take her out for a walk. Aunt Mary had crocheted a blanket and snowsuit for Suzie, my doll. Aunt Mary told my mother and father to make sure that they told me. She was helping Santa Claus out that year. There was so much excitement in our house that morning; I almost forgot my stocking that I had carefully hung on the mantle the night before. After opening a present of a clown bank that opened his mouth when I pulled the lever, I remembered my Christmas stocking. It was really my stocking. It was cotton. We did not have ornate Christmas stockings that are bought at stores. They were ours. Every year the stocking would contain some coins, which usually were stuck to the hard Christmas candy that was part of the assortment in the toe part. There was a tangerine. I remember tangerines being so delicious at Christmastime. It held figs and dates more carefully wrapped than the hard candy in the toe. We had these things around the house every Christmas. The men that worked for my father brought them to us; however, this was very personal. The contents of my stocking were mine alone. There were some little things for Suzie also. There was a doll baby bottle and nipple. There was a tiny pacifier. There were doll shoes and stockings. My Christmas stocking was topped off with a banana and a plum.

We finished opening our presents and then went upstairs in order to get dressed in our new Christmas clothing. We attended the nine a.m. children's Mass at Sacred Heart of Jesus Church. Sacred Heart of Jesus Church was the mecca of culture. There were the paintings of the saints and angels on the ceiling. The Blessed Mother had an altar on the left hand side of the church. Saint Joseph's altar stood on the right hand side of the church. The Crucifixion was in the middle of the large marble middle altar. There were marble pillars throughout the church. On one side of each marble pillar was a blue glass panel that held a bright light inside. It emitted a beautiful hue. On the left hand side of the walls and the right hand side of the walls were the fourteen Stations of the Cross, artistically designed and sculptured. There were stained glass windows of the angels and the saints. The Mass was said in Latin and I learned Latin immediately when I was in first grade. In fact, some of the people in our neighborhood spoke Latin much more literate than they did English. The choir sang angelically that Christmas morning. The memory of the little angel who was taken back to heaven because she could not stop eating Mrs. Parker's cookies came into my head. I named her Mai, pronounced My. I visualized her singing and dancing in heaven. I thought of Mrs. Parker's cookies.

🕊 🕊 🕊 🕊 🕊 🕊 🕊 🕊

Adeste fideles, laeti triumphtes,	O come, all ye faithful, joyful and triumphant
Veni te, veni te in Bethlehem	Come ye, O come ye to Bethlehem
Natum videte,	Come and behold him,
Regem angelorum	Born the King of angels
Venite adoremus,	O come, let us adore him,
Venite adoremus	O come, let us adore him,
Do minum	Christ the Lord!

John F. Wade, ca. 1711-1786, tr. by Frederick Oakeley, 1802-1880, alt. Music: John F. Wade

The choir burst into a rendition of Hark! The Herald Angels Sing

Hark the herald angels sing:
"Glory to the newborn King;
Peace on earth, and mercy mild,
God and sinners reconcilled

Charles Wesley, 1707-1788, alt.
Music: Felix Mendelssohn 1809-1847; arr. by William H. Cummings, 1831-1915

It sounded so idyllic. Roosevelt by now had lent Britain money for supplies. Britain had little money of its own for arms and supplies. Roosevelt strived for peace on earth and good will toward men. History indicates that Roosevelt proclaimed neutrality.

I was all involved in my own little world but I could not help wondering what was going on out in the world. Something big was going on; I just did not know what. I knew people took sides, I knew that even before FDR was elected for his third term.

The City of Philadelphia was very Republican in the 1940s. My father was Republican. My father was a Committeeman. My Uncle John was a Democrat. Bobby and I went to the Mooneys' house because my mother had a doctor's appointment. Marie was in school. Uncle John seized the moment. He said, "I'm going to teach you a little ditty." I want you to say it at supper tonight. If you get it right, I will give you both a nickel. Cachinga! I will get it right. I knew Bobby would get it right also. He was smart like me. Here is what Uncle John told us to say at supper when my father was there:

♪ ♪ ♪ ♪ ♪ ♪ ♪ ♪

Roosevelt, Roosevelt, ring the bell
Wilke, Wilke go to hell

♪ ♪ ♪ ♪ ♪ ♪ ♪ ♪

Uncle John would have liked to have been there with a camera when the moment came. Daddy asked us questions at supper. He asked me what was new. I said Bobby and I know a new saying. He said, "Let's hear it." I said "Okay." At first when Uncle John coached me, I was not too sure about the h word. Then I realized about good and evil and Sister Edna and the priests said it in certain contexts. The Devil was in hell. Maybe Wilke was a bad man. Since I was going to have another nickel for my cigar box, I justified the use of the h word. Therefore, I asked Bobby if he would like to recite our new ditty. He said, "No." I knew he had apprehension about using the h word. I do not think he ever used it. I suggested we say it in unison. He was too unsure of the moral implications of saying hell. I said, "Okay, I'll recite it." Daddy said, "Well come on, somebody recite it." Okay, here goes:

Roosevelt, Roosevelt, ring the bell
Wilke, Wilke, go to hell

Daddy blurted out, "I'll be go to hell." My conscience was clear. I would not want to sell my soul for a nickel. Therefore, daddy's response relieved me. He regained his composure and asked where we learned that. Bobby kept shoving his food into his mouth. He could not answer with a mouthful of food. I hesitated, I was not a snitch; especially, when it involved Uncle John, who was a good uncle and I loved him. I told him I heard some man say it on Third Street. He asked me what I was doing on Third Street. Mother interjected to renew his memory that she took us to Aunt Alice and Uncle John's house because she was taking Andy to the doctor. Marie was in school. That was the end of the questioning. He repeated, "I'll be go to hell." He had asked me a question, and I answered without telling a lie and without being a snitch.

After Christmas break that year, we got down to brass tacks or business in first grade. Sister Mary Edna started to talk about the Pagan babies. She said there were Pagan babies that never heard of Jesus. We must sacrifice and send nickels and dimes to the missionaries that were going to tell them about Jesus. She showed us pictures of them. They were naked and lived in a tropical setting. They seemed happy, they just did not know about Jesus. Sister Edna went all out for the Pagan babies. She had an elaborate China box that sat on her desk. It had a gold crucifix attached to it. It had a small statue of a Pagan Baby holding onto the box. The slot on it was for the donations to the Pagan babies. I took it serious and put a coin in there when I could. I often sacrificed a pretzel. I thought it was more important to help my cousin Joe out by buying him a pretzel. He sat right in the same room with me. His father had died several months before Joe was born. His mother Aunt Winnie was a very proud British woman. There was only a social program called Mothers' Assistance as I recall. It was only a stipend. I knew that Joe did not have money for pretzels, I preferred on most days to buy one for him as the Pagan babies looked like they were happy being naked and not knowing Jesus.

The money was not coming in fast enough for Sister Edna. She put out a mandate. Anyone who drops his or her pretzel money loses it. It goes right into the Pagan baby box. We were only babies. I took my nickels serious. Now the logistics were good. Sister Mary Edna stood by the first desk at the second row of desks. We were to line up in the second row in order to get our pretzel. We were then to proceed up the first aisle in order to return to our seats. I got right up to her. As she was about to hand me my pretzel, I dropped my nickel. She picked it up and plopped it right into the box for the Pagan babies. I held my right hand out and demanded, "One pretzel, please." She responded, "No, go to your seat. Your nickel will go to the Pagan babies; the missionaries can then teach them about Jesus." I did not say anything but I was thinking. Here it was a bitter cold winter day in Philadelphia, Pennsylvania. The Pagan babies are in some area of the world running <soopsu> naked and enjoying the tropical setting. <Ta> Then, I proceeded to go to the first aisle as directed; only I went right out that door. I did not bother to get my coat. I did not have time. I had to take it on the lam fast. I heard that line in the gangster movie. Timing was just as important as logistics. My cousin Nuny Wootten was assigned to open the window on the third floor. She was in eighth grade. Her eyes almost bulged out of her head. She started screaming, "Sister, sister, my baby cousin is walking down Moyamensing Avenue, crossing streets without a coat." "Hurry, hurry," the nun said, "Go get her." Nuny donned her gray tweed winter coat and ran as fast as she could. She ran so fast that I was only up to little Wilder Street when she caught up with me. She asked me what happened. She then told me to get under her coat before I told her. We looked so funny zigzagging south on Moyamensing Avenue. I told her that I would not accept that nonsense. I explained how I felt about the Pagan babies. I thought on this particular blustery day, they were better off than we were. They were running around naked in a tropical setting. It is not my fault that they do not know Jesus. She consoled me and told me that the nuns always talk about the Pagan babies. "Why did you leave school without a coat because of the Pagan babies?" I said in my own words, "It was the principle of the thing. I dropped my nickel. Sister put it in the Pagan baby box, I did not get my pretzel; I did not have any to share with Joe, and it is not fair. I want my nickel back. If I give to the Pagan babies of my own will, that is okay. I don't have anything against the Pagan babies; however, when a kid doesn't want to give her nickel to the Pagan babies, she shouldn't be forced to give her nickel up to them." Nuny and I arrived home just as my mother was starting to cook the dittalinis. She asked Nuny to stay and eat with us. Nuny did that often. She was like a guardian angel to me. Mother looked and said, "Glory be, what happened? Where's your coat, Joan?" I asked Nuny to explain it, as I was too tired from the trauma of the day. Nuny told her. Mother said, "Oh, dear, I suppose I'll take her back to school for the afternoon session. I need to talk to Sister Mary Edna." Of course, it would not be a confrontation. Sister was always right. I slept for fifteen minutes, before I ate my dittalinis smothered with cheese and tomato sauce. I dressed in my Sunday coat and Mother took me to the convent. Mother timed it so she would not be intruding. We arrived shortly before the nuns were to cross Moyamensing Avenue from the convent to the school for the afternoon session. Mother rang the bell. Sister Augusta answered. I loved Sister Augusta and it gave me some hope. I would be getting her in second grade, hopefully, if I survive first grade. Sister Augusta summoned Sister Mary Edna. She explained that she thought I went back to my desk. When she discovered I was not there and was gone for some time, she sent someone to look for me. People usually did not snatch kids in those days. The eighth grade nun sent a brownie from eighth grade to give Sister Mary Edna the message that I was with Catherine Wootten, unharmed.

Sister Mary Edna looked down at me because I was the smaller. She said, "Dear, come back to school. Today, we're going to learn about Adam and Eve." This was too good to pass up, so I agreed. She thanked my mother for bringing me to the convent than looked at me and said, "God bless you dear." I put out my right hand and asked her if I may have my nickel back. She complied. It went right into my cigar box when I came home from school that day. She had not realized, I was business minded and had three businesses even before I started school.

CHAPTER 14

Sister told us about Adam and Eve and the Garden of Eden. Everybody was in a tropical setting except us. I already learned from the Baltimore Catechism why God made me. I was supposed to know him to love him and to serve him in this world. Then I would be happy with him forever in the next. That was very understandable. But wait, the plot thickens. There are three people in one God. The Father, the Son and the Holy Ghost. We said Ghost back then, now it is Spirit. It was a mystery. I thought well maybe Mr. Mahoney, who was a detective, could solve it. But no! It was deeper than that. It had to do with faith. Okay, I already knew my Apostles' Creed.

What I did not get was the entire Genesis story. God created the world in six days. On the seventh day, he rested. He put Adam and Eve in the Garden of Eden. They were not allowed to eat apples. They could have anything else their hearts desired. It was idyllic. A snake came around and told Eve to tell Adam to bite the apple. Eve went to Adam and told him to bite the apple. I knew at that moment if one of my ribs started talking to me, I would just pretend I did not even hear it and go about my business. Now what I did not understand among many other things was why God put the apple tree there if they could not eat the apples. Why was Adam such a pansy? Why didn't he leave that God damned apple alone? Then what would you expect from one of your ribs talking to you? I did not like being born with a sin that I did not enjoy committing.

It did cross my mind that if God put my brother Bobby there in the garden, he may not pass the test. Bobby loves apples to this day. He even let the family skeleton out of the closet by announcing, "Hooray, hooray, today's apple day when Aunt Mary and Uncle Sam were on public assistance called welfare or relief. Bobby was good. He always strived to reason things out in order to make the right decisions. He was not a patsy for anyone. He just had a good, strong character. When Aunt Mary would try to send him to the store to get two cents worth of bologna, cut thin, he would say, "Aunt Mary, I'll be back. I'm in the middle of something right now." Usually he was in the middle of thinking it would be embarrassing to go to the store and ask for two cents worth of bologna, especially since everyone knew we were a family of six in the early forties. Two cents worth of bologna, for a family of six. How cheap! I do not think they would have been able to cut it that thin. Bobby was not lying to Aunt Mary. He did go back, after he was sure she found some other kid to go buy her two cents worth of bologna, cut thin.

However, I knew that if God Himself told Bobby not to eat the God dammed apple, he would not. I just knew that about Bobby. I raised my hand three or four times and asked Sister Edna questions, such as: "If God was God why did he set that scene up in the first place?" She said, "They needed to show they trusted God." I asked, "Why?" She said because then they would know God, love God, serve God in Eden, and be happy with Him forever in heaven. I said, "Sister, it sounded like they were already in heaven." She said, "No, they weren't; heaven is the Beautific Vision." It was getting too deep for me, but I wanted more answers. I liked that Christ was born. Oh, Christmas was heavenly. I guess in retrospect God's gift to us at Christmas is that we get a spiritual glimpse of how the Beautific Vision feels. What I did not like was the Crucifixion. I would look up at Jesus hanging on the cross and see my father or my cousins or my uncles who were really my cousins. I did not like that at all. I did not want Christ to have had to go through all that. There is no symbolism in the Crucifixion. It is real. Later in life, I learned about symbolism in the Garden of Eden. After my third question, Sister Mary Edna stood by my desk. I thought <atta> no, here come those scissors again. To my surprise, she held out the biggest lollipop I had ever seen. I thought I am so bright she wants to reward me. The lollipop was white with red, gold, blue, green and purple extending from the center. It reminded me of a windmill ornament. I could not resist opening it. She said something very strange as I was opening it. She said, "You will be introduced to Phil O'Sophical debaiting in higher education." I was looking forward to meeting this Irish guy when I entered second grade. I listened intently while Sister Mary Edna taught more about Adam and Eve. Some questions entered my mind, but I was enjoying my lollipop so much that I did not bother to ask them; besides, I already had received the lollipop for being so bright.

My cousin Jimmy Wootten was drafted. It was peacetime. It was the first peacetime draft in American history. It was set up in September of 1940. In March 1941, Congress passed the Lend Lease Act. The act allowed FDR to sell or lend war materials to any country whose defense the President deemed vital to the defense of the United States. He said under the Lend lease act America would become the arsenal of democracy. Our four freedoms would be defended: freedom of speech and worship and freedom from want and fear.

My cousin was somewhere far away and would not be able to come and see me in the May procession. Sacred Heart had all the pomp and circumstances for every event. The May Queen was voted to be May Queen by her schoolmates in the eighth grade. She then had a May Court of two children from the first grade, eventually the court increased from two to eight. Usually the brownies served on the court when it was two. The entire school population participated in the May procession. The girls wore white. The second grade children had made their Holy Communion that morning. They wore their entire ensemble and carried their First Holy Communion books, which were given to them by Father Walsh. First grade processed behind the communicants. The first grade girls carried a little white basket of daises to strew as they walked up the aisles; the choir sang Blessed Mother hymns.

ഗ•ഗ•ഗ•ഗ•ഗ•ഗ•ഗ•ഗ

On this day, O beautiful Mother

On this day, O beautiful Mother,
On this day we give thee our love.
Near thee, Madonna, fondly we hover,
Trusting thy gentle care to prove.

Rohr's Favorite Catholic Melodies, 1857. Music: Louis Lambillotte, Sj,
1796-1855

Despite the distractions of the <wo!> oh and ahs, here come the babies, I never forgot the feeling that I had that day. I know spirituality when it hits me. I sure knew it that day. I just wished that my cousin Jimmy could have been there to see me.

CHAPTER 15

"You're it," echoed throughout Sacred Heart schoolyard at recess time. There were two different teams. "You're it," was heard throughout the entire fifteen minutes of recess. I never was tagged. However, on my way home, I saw a bus go by; it had a big picture of the Uncle Sam that stands for the United States of America. I did not know the connection between the picture and the USA on that particular day. Since I was not tagged, I felt shrewd. Then this bus went by, a man called Uncle Sam pointed his finger and said, "I want you." Chez and crackers, I cannot hide from God. I cannot hide from the "You're it" tag team, because they would go and tell somebody in government. Then, a bus would go by and say, "I want you." It was enough to make a person paranoid if a person was not already inclined in that direction in the first place. I crossed Moyamensing Avenue with the guidance of the Safety Patrol. I then crossed Reed Street again with the guidance of the Safety Patrol. I passed Sacred Heart of Jesus Church and blessed myself. That is what we were taught to do and besides I really loved to say hello to Jesus, Mary and Saint Joseph and all the angels and saints. We now crossed little Gerritt Street. Little Gerritt Street was smaller than any street I had ever seen. It was smaller than the historic Elfreths Alley was. I had three friends with me: Peggy Banning, MaryAnn Nesko and Anna Muldowney. We then passed Rodgers funeral home. If a crepe was on the door, we paused and said, "God rest their soul." That is what Aunt Mary said when she spoke of a deceased person, whether she liked them or not. We proceeded south on Moyamensing Avenue. We passed the creepy looking Seafarers' Institute. It was a big, big building. It was always painted blue around the framework on the doors and windows. It loomed as if to say, "Stay away." We then proceeded to Dickinson Street. The Safety Patrol crossed us on Dickinson Street, then again on Moyamensing Avenue. Our next stop was the First District Police Station. We went in for a drink of water. The police officers use to tease us. They put pictures of police officers over the water cooler. On top of one police officer's picture was typed, WANTED; underneath was typed, REWARD one fishcake. There were other funny rewards as well. However, that one hit me in the eye. I laughed; who would try to apprehend someone for a fishcake? Now, I thought maybe if it were a nickel. The police officer behind the desk asked us how school was going. If we had any school news, we would tell them. Usually our responses were "Okay." By now, first grade was preparing for final exams. That was on my mind. I certainly was not going to discuss my apprehension about it with those police officers. I was leery of everyone. I needed time to think it over. I decided it was safe to discuss my final exams with them. I was so happy I did, as some of them went to Catholic school and remembered the trick questions such as, "If there were three pieces of fruit on the table and one banana and one orange and one apple rolled of the table, how many pieces of fruit would be left on the table?" I asked, "What kind of question is that, a banana can't roll?" The police officer said it was just an example; keep your eyes and mind open.

I had so much on my mind that May of 1940. My cousin Jimmy was in France. By May, the Germans had trapped the Allies at Dunkirk on the English Channel. The British sent every available warship, merchant ship, even fishing and pleasure boats to rescue the trapped soldiers. They carried over 330,000 English and French soldiers to safety in England. German armies then marched on Paris. On June 22, 1940, France surrendered. I was so concerned about Jimmy, I prayed extra hard.

I remembered what the police officer told me about trick questions. When the final exams came, I scrutinize every question. I received a score of ninety-six. I passed first grade; No more pencils, no more books, no more Pagan babies for three entire months. I was going to be in Sister Augusta's class. I prayed and prayed that she would not be transferred from Sacred Heart to another Catholic parish; and she was not.

Summer began; I slept in until ten a.m. I should have been treated for posttraumatic stress disorder, but they did not have such names for things then. The sleeping until I was ready to get out of bed and the fresh fruits and vegetables that I ate eventually restored me. By the Fourth of July, I was springing out of bed by eight a.m. The Fourth of July was an extravaganza in our neighborhood. The vacant lot across the street from our house was cleaned up. A hot dog stand was set up. Homemade root beer came out of a barrel. There were potato chips and games and a seesaw was set up for the kids to play on if they desired. There was a sliding board. There were games that enticed one to participate because prizes were given out to the winners. There was the potato sack race. A kid would get into the potato sack, which usually covered much of the thighs. They would then run in the potato sack. Not easy, but someone always won. Then there was the blueberry pie-eating contest. There was an egg fight. That was too messy for me; however, some brave souls did participate. That Fourth of July in 1941 was so eventful and we had so much fun. Usually my parents would take us to Independence Hall where the Liberty Bell stood. Presidents and dignitaries were the orators. It was a good such a good, patriotic feeling to know that we live in this great USA. There was extraordinary patriotism all over historic Philadelphia. We called it Independence Day. We visited the Betsy Ross house. The first American flag was made by Betsy in the garden next to her house. She went to church with George Washington and his family and many other American patriots.

★ ★ ★ ★ ★ ★ ★ ★ ★ ★ ★ ★ ★

America The Beautiful

O beautiful for spacious skies,
For amber waves of grain,
For purple mountain majesties
Above the fruited plain!
America! America! God shed his grace on thee,
And crown thy good with brotherhood
From sea to shining sea.

Katherine L. Bates, 1859-1929, Music: Samuel A. Ward 1848-1903

It seemed as though September came in a blink of an eye. It was a fun summer. I had good friends such as Doris Gregory, Marion Egger, Peggy Banning, Flossie Stockman, Jeanne Lloyd, Aggie Winters, Doris Matonis and all the friends I had from swimmies. Some of these friends were publics. The publics went to Abigal Vare public School. It was located at Moyamensing Avenue and Morris Street. I knew that I would not be seeing much of the publics over the winter. I did not fret because I knew summer would be back in the blink of an eye and then we would hang out together again. We would put on plays, just as Sacred Heart did.

We liked to play Gypsies in our Summer Playhouse, which was the yard of someone's house.

Sacred Heart always had plays, musicals and movies of the Pagan babies in their fourth floor auditorium. I liked to go because then I could really see how the Pagan babies really lived. I did not see one of them with the Jensen's Violet on their skins from ringworms. I did not see a school nurse coming in and checking their heads for lice or nits. Every time I saw that school nurse come into our class, my head started to itch. She never found cooties or nits on me. My father made sure of that. He had us lean over the sink in the bathroom and go over our heads with a fine-toothed comb. That way if there were any adult cooties, they would come marching out. That was the easy part. He then had steel like nit-comb, which reminded me of a razor head that I had seen at the barbershop when I went with my father. I did not like that nit-comb. However, one day when I was six my Aunt Mary took me up town to have my hair permed. It was as if someone died. The hair stylists formed a little circle. They needed to decide what to do. They knew Aunt Mary was Lace Curtains Irish and she always left a nice tip for them. I was just waiting and observing. The perm apparatus looked like they were getting ready to send someone out of space. It had wires attached to the curlers, which was some type of tin. It looked like sheer torture.

"Okay," they agreed. The consensus was that they would have to tell Aunt Mary that they could not perm my hair that day because they found some nits. "WHAT, WHAT? We are Lace Curtain Irish. Never, Never." The technician tried to reason with Aunt Mary. She said that maybe she was playing with someone who has cooties.

That calmed Aunt Mary down some. Now it would not be proper for my parents to check for cooties on the heads of my playmates before I could play with them. Daddy started the regimen of going over our heads with a fine-toothed comb and then a nit-comb. He prided himself on it. I was so happy that I did not have to be wired to that machine, that the inconvenience of having my head scrutinized several times a week was a small price to pay. Even though my father fine-toothed combed our heads several times a week, my head still itched every time I saw the school nurse come into the classroom to check for cooties. She used a stick just as Sister Mary Edna used to put on Donald Coleman's tongue when he fell out of the desk on the first day of school. The school nurse's stick did not have cotton wrapped around it. It still made me itch. The next day after the nurse examined our heads, one or two children came to school with their heads shaved. It was not their fault; they must have been playing with some other children who had their cooties jumping into the bald kids heads before their heads were shaved bald.

My father occasionally went to the barbershop for a shave and a haircut. Usually, he shaved himself. After his hair was cut, the barber used Burma Shave to prep my father's face. "Shave and a haircut, two bits," was the saying in our neighborhood. I do not know if that is what the charge was or it just sounded cool for the kids to recite. Burma Shave always had huge signs on the highways. When we went down to The Atlantic Seashore, in New Jersey, we always looked forward to spotting the Burma Shave signs and reciting them aloud. Some I still remember. They usually had a good message such as, "He saw the train and tried to duck it, kicked first the gas and then the bucket." Burma Shave.

In August of 1941, President Roosevelt and Prime Minister Churchill issued the Atlantic Charter. The charter set up goals for the postwar world. In it, the two leaders agreed to seek no territorial gain. They pledged to support "the right of all peoples to choose the form of government under which they will live." The charter also called for a "permanent system of general security."

In August of 1941, Aunt Mary took me to Strawbridge and Clothier, the grand department store that was very sophisticated. Salespeople were required to wear dark sophisticated colors. Women who worked there wore high heels and never went without stockings. At Christmastime, the windows of Strawbridge and Clothier were transformed into Dicken's Christmas Carol scenes. There were little houses with animated figures. There were Tiny Tim and the entire Crachit family. There was a big goose on the table. Ebenezer Scrooge was smiling in the background. There was always a fireplace. There was an entire village. It had a bakery shoppe, a church and a bank plus every type of building that a quaint little village would contain.

Aunt Mary took me before school began. She always bought my shoes. She was my godmother.

CHAPTER 16

I was enthused because by now I knew Sister Mary Augusta was not transferred from Sacred Heart School to another parochial school. I will never ever forget Sister Augusta. I do not think she realized at the start of the 1941-1942 school year, that she would be required to play so many roles. Sister Mary Augusta was an upbeat nun, and she loved the children. She introduced us to the courses we would be learning in the second grade. I never did meet that Irish guy, Phil O' Sophical who was debating. Everything about him puzzled me when Sister Mary Edna first said I would be introduced to him in higher education. Never, ever did I see a bug, or a mouse or even a flea in any of Sacred Heart of Jesus buildings? <A>. Maybe he was supposed to exterminate the cooties from the heads of the children that the nurse deemed necessary. Maybe he was drafted.

The mad exterminators in Europe were still marching, sending innocent people to the gas chambers. The stories were leaking out. I could not decipher whether they were true or not. As I recall, the newscasters were not broadcasting Hitler sent Jews, Poles, Gypsies and even Catholic priests to the gas chambers. I took it with a grain of salt. I was used to hearing strange stories in our neighborhood. He targeted the midgets. In retrospect, I can tell you the midgets in our neighborhood were giants of men and women. I was happy I met Emma Jane again before she died in the late 1900s. She was such a good person. She had lost her son suddenly about a decade before she died. It did not embitter her. She used her grief to help other people. If someone had a tragedy, Emma Jane would be right at their door to console them. Emma Jane had the gift of reaching out to other people to help heal them. Rest in peace, Emma Jane; you were a giant of a woman.

I remembered what my friend Anna told me about Warsaw in 1939. Some of her relatives were fortunate enough to get out of Poland. The entire thing going on over there was too incomprehensible to grasp. I tried to think things through but I would not be reaching the age of reason until December 1941. I thought if they come after Sylvia, I would stand in front of her and tell Hitler to take me. Then I could bask in heaven with the angels and saints including, Saint Joan of Arc. Sylvia was one of the most beautiful people I ever knew, both on the outside and on the inside.

She was tan and slim. Her mother Shirley dressed to the nines on Friday and Saturday evenings and went to a nightclub uptown called The Latin Casino. I use to think, how could Shirley and Manny produce such a beautiful creature like Sylvia. I knew one thing; no matter what, the maniacs would never get to my friend Sylvia or any of her family. I would make sure of that. Unlike Saint Joan of Arc, who was burned at the stake, I probably would get the bayonet; however, it could still be considered grounds for sainthood. I wondered what I would be called as sleep overtook me amidst the wonderings of my saintly names, Saint Joan of the South Philly waterfront. Saint Joan, lover of Jews. I thought it could not be Saint Joan, lover of Jews. I would not let them hurt anyone. Saint Joan of the Gypsies did not sound right to me; besides, it would be a conflict of interest. We were taught that it was a sin to read crystal balls. I heard about all the people that he was after and I thought it would have to be simply: Saint Joan of Sacred Heart School, in the heart of South Philly. It would make them proud of me. I drifted off to sleep with the saintly name I had selected. I did have a couple of last thoughts before I drifted off to the world of milk and honey, where a good person goes when they fall asleep. I decided that I would stand in front of the Chinese. I would stand in front of any other human being. I would not let them get to anyone before they went through me first. The nuns taught me that I would be assured of going to heaven if I boiled in hot oil. Sometimes, the lions would have to eat me. It did not go together. The lions would not get me already fried in hot oil. They were two different types of martyrdom.

The sound of my father's alarm clock awakened me at five a.m. the next morning. He had station WIP on the radio. I just wished they would not be broadcasting that loud. In the early evening, we used to listen to Uncle WIP. He was so nice. On my birthday, that year, he announced, Joan Morrisroe look under the cushion of the sofa and you will discover something nice for your birthday. I was in awe. Joan Morrisroe, he said. Now, I was on the airwaves even before I was boiled in oil or torn apart and eaten by the lions of the Roman arenas. I looked under the cushion of the sofa. There was a silkworm set. The larva of a silkworm excretes a substance resembling silk. It eventually turns into a moth.

The night before school began for the 1941-1942 semesters, I was so excited about having Sister Augusta as my teacher. I had a little time to think before I finally fell asleep. I knew things were happening but I did not know exactly what. Then, I was used to secrets. How could I figure out what was going on in the entire world when I still had the mystery of the Rittenhouse family on my mind. I visualized how I would look in my new first day of school outfit. My hair was cut short. It took Aunt Mary several years to get over the N word. That stood for nits in those days. Things change. Time marches on and what once was often is not anymore.

I went to school willingly. I did not have anybody who was "on" and then went "off" and forgot a little kid. I loved Sister Augusta. She called us girls her little rosebuds. She said we all smelled like little rose buds. Almost everybody got a bath in preparation for the first day of school. Sister Augusta asked us our names, one by one, in alphabetical order. She then wrote each name on the blackboard with the white chalk. I loved to see my name on the blackboard. It made me feel so special. I knew that she was a fair nun, as the usual brownie was not answering the door. The little girl assigned to answer the door was a kid that had been pushed in the back of the classroom in an aisle of desks closest to the windows, as far away from the door as possible. However, that was history now. We had Sister Augusta and she was a fair nun. She also was a kind nun. She still looked on us as her babies, however the mantra for second grade, was officially, "Second grade, rats." However, not in Sister Augusta's class. She pampered us and gave us gifts. It was a fair game in second grade. We started to lose our baby teeth. If someone lost a tooth, a present was received from Sister Augusta. I went to school one Friday morning of late September. My tooth was loose. Oh, please God, let it fall out while school is in session. Then Sister Augusta would reward me. After we bought our pretzels and I made sure my cousin Joe had a pretzel, we followed Sister Augusta's instructions to lay our heads down on the desk for ten minutes. I complied. I started to play with my loose tooth. It fell out. Sister Augusta did not have the usual rewards for the loss of our baby teeth. She was all out. Business was booming. A tooth here, a tooth there, here a tooth, there a tooth, E I E I O. I put my head up from the naptime and she knew I had lost a tooth. It was a tooth in the front of my mouth. There was a little blood, she stood at my desk and wiped it off with a tissue. She carefully wrapped my tooth in another tissue and handed it back to me in order to double dip with the tooth fairy that night when I went to bed. I would then put it under my pillow until the tooth fairy came and took it. The tooth fairy usually left me a nickel. You see, I was not a novice at this. I already had lost one tooth previously. Since Sister Augusta was a fair nun and she was out of Hershey bars or treats of any type, she handed me a nickel. Cachinga!

I liked what I was learning in second grade. My writing was getting more like the writing I first saw when I entered first grade. I learned higher numbers. I learned poetry.

Sister Augusta read bible history to us on Friday afternoons. I would not miss Friday afternoons unless I had the Scarlet fever or something that would quarantine me. Then a big sign would be put in our front window on the left sign that read, QUARANTINED. That is how they did the infectious diseases in the 1940s. I liked the pictures I saw in our bible history books. Jerusalem, Nazareth, Bethlehem. Everyone was tan. I remember the photos in the book were bright colors. I liked to hear the stories. Sister Augusta did not go over Genesis again. We already learned that in first grade. I especially liked how she presented the information. Sister Augusta could present any material in a positive, good light. That is how she was. She had no hidden agenda. She cared more for her second grade babies than the Pagan babies. I do not ever remember her taking any of the kid's money when they did not want to give it up in the first place. She was a giver, not a taker. Sacred Heart parish had social programs of its own. The Reverend Henry V. Walsh was pastor. There were various opinions of the Reverend Henry V. Walsh. I myself found him intimidating. People complained about his haughty demeanor, not to his face, of course. Moreover, I do not mean the alcoholics that would gather in the bars and complain about Father Walsh asking for money all the time, as they were strewing their week's wages in the bar. Their children would then have to be fed by Father Walsh. He implemented a program whereby a child who did not have breakfast at home would be fed hot food at recess time. There was no fuss made. The recess bell rang and we would form two lines. One was to go to breakfast. One was to go to the schoolyard. Sister Augusta saw I was white like China, she told me to go to the breakfast. The nuns always asked me if I drank enough milk because I was white like China. I would pass my sister Marie who was in fourth grade. She yelled, "I'm telling mommy and daddy, little twerp." We ate breakfast together this morning. "I'm telling, I'm telling." {So, tell I thought what do you want me to do, hold a Shiva for you?} I heard Manny say that to Shirley when she complained. Sister Augusta told me to go but I did not tell Marie that. It was nobody's business but my own. She did, she told. She could not wait to get home to tell. When my mother went to open house at Sacred Heart School, she talked to Sister Augusta. She said Marie told them that I was going to the free hot breakfast every morning. Sister Augusta said, "Yes, I told her to go." Mother told her that I ate a hot breakfast at home before I left for school. Sister Augusta said, "She is so white. I think it's good if she eats a hot breakfast again in mid morning." Sister Augusta had diagnosed my hypoglycemia before any medical doctor. She did not realize that is why I was so white. I liked the story she read, "Snow White and the Seven Dwarfs." It gave me some things to ponder. I did not challenge it, although it sounded like a nightmare to me even when I was read the story before I started school. Snow White had to deal with all those different personalities. I would not want a grumpy little dwarf around me.

The United States tried to stop Japanese aggression by cutting off the sale of oil and scrap metal to Japan. These moves angered the Japanese because they badly needed the oil and the metal. In November 1941, Japanese and American officials tried to settle it peacefully. Japan wanted the United States to lift the embargo on oil and scrap metal. The United States wanted Japan to withdraw its armies from China and Southeast Asia. Neither side would compromise. Therefore, the talks broke off. Japan planned a secret attack on the USA.

Our Christmas pageant was scheduled for December 7, 1941. Everyone liked to see the second graders perform. A professional make-up artist made us up to play the various assigned roles in the Christmas pageant. It was to be held in the basement of Sacred Heart School. It was a social hall. We had a makeshift stage. I was assigned to be Saint Joseph. Wow! Saint Joseph himself. We rehearsed perfectly. Finally, I would reach the age of reason on December 6, 1941. Little did I realize how important it was to have the capability to reason the events of Sunday, December 7, 1941.

I had my role of Saint Joseph down pat. I went to sleep anticipating the crowd would be large and the applause would include people standing up chanting, "Bravo." I worked hard. I knew my lines perfectly. I was abruptly awakened at eight-fifteen a.m. That was the usual time I arose. However, it was not with all the fanfare. Our little Philco radio was blasting the news: At seven fifty-five a.m. on this peaceful Sunday morning, Japanese planes appeared in the sky over Pearl Harbor, Hawaii. The United States Pacific fleet sat peacefully in the harbor below. The Japanese are bombing them. Americans were stunned! The attack continued for over two hours. The Japanese bombs sank or seriously damaged nineteen American ships, destroyed 150 American planes, and killed about 2,400 people. Fortunately, for the United States all three aircraft carriers of its Pacific fleet were at sea. What does it mean? "We'll find out," was everyone's response. People were in and out of our house. I went to nine a.m. Mass but I was uneasy. I did not know what that news meant. I felt relieved when I went to church. We sang the usual hymns and retorts in Latin. We sang:

CBCBCBCBCBCBCBCB
Mary Help Us, Help We Pray

Mary Help Us, help we pray.
Help your children night and day.
Keep them from all harm and sorrow.
Mary help us, help we pray.

CBCBCBCBCBCBCBCB

The Arizona at Pearl Harbor, December 7, 1941-

CHAPTER 17

I did not feel hungry. I felt scared. Nobody could tell me what it meant. Actually, the adults were as confused and stunned as I was. I remember pulling my mother's coat until it came off the hook in the closet leading to the cellar. It was bright orange. It had a big fur collar, almost as big as I was. I went behind the sofa and hid under the coat. The fur was my pillow. {Oh dear, what does it mean, what does it mean?} My cousin Richie Wootten came into our house. People were in and out of each other's houses all over the neighborhood. Other people came into our house. I was scared. What does it mean? Richie was my cousin. He was eligible for the draft. He always came into our house, as did our dozens of other relatives in the neighborhood. He was walking to the kitchen where most of our family was gathered for breakfast. Nobody ate much. I was even too scared to go to breakfast. We had a skylight window in the ceiling of the breakfast room. I visualized the Japanese dropping bombs through it. I was not only scared of the Japanese because they looked different; I was scared because they were evil. Richie spied the little ball of me wrapped up behind the sofa. The sofa was alongside of the fireplace. The back was not against a wall or anything. My mother had it set up like a nice cozy sitting area. Richie looked and said, "What do we have here?" He picked up the little ball of wool and fur. My eyes were peeping out of it. He said, "What's the matter Nicholena?" He always called me Nicholena because I was born on the feast day of Saint Nicholas. I mumbled, "I'm scared." He said, "WHAT?" He uncovered my mouth. By now, the tears

155

were running down my face. I said, "I'm scared." He replied, "I will never, ever let anyone hurt you in any way. Do you understand that, my little Nicholena?" I said, "Yes." He then removed the coat from my tiny body and carried me into the kitchen to join the family for breakfast. My mother said, "Joan, make sure you eat and you'll have another little snack before you go to your pageant." {Oh, no!} For a while, I even forgot my pageant. This was serious. Dinner was going to be served that Sunday at four p.m. because the Christmas pageant was scheduled for two p.m.

My father drove us to Sacred Heart School. My mother wore diamond earrings from Woolworth 5 &10 store. They shined in the dark. I summoned everything I had ever learned about good character: ethics, faith, hope, and charity and aspirations such as, "My Jesus mercy" then went to the kitchen of Sacred Heart School. The make up artist was applying the various applications for the Nativity roles. We had costumes. My mother said if she did not know what role I was playing, she would not have recognized me. I made sure I kept my eyes on her earrings, throughout the pageant. Even when the lights went off, I could see her earrings shining. That gave me some security. The curtain opened. The scenery was set. The donkey was composed of a donkey costume with a girl in front and a girl in the rear. Two girls and a donkey costume made the donkey that took Mary from Nazareth to Bethlehem. Mary was sitting on the donkey. I stood by her with my staff. Mary said, "Joseph, we need to find lodging, I believe the time has come to deliver Jesus our Savior into the world." I said, "Okay Mary. We will stop at the inn." Bethlehem was so over crowed that year that the innkeeper told them that there was no room at the inn. I had my lines down perfectly. He did suggest lodging in a stable. Nothing else was available. At least a stable would provide some shelter. We approached the stable. I knocked on the door of the stable. My friend Gail was playing the part of the stable owner. She had rehearsed, "Yes, come in, you can have lodging here." With all due respect to Gail, I think the happenings of the day had her off course, as it did me. I did not forget my lines; however, thank God. Gail said, "No, we have no lodging here." {Oh dear, what to do, what to do?} I can reason. I am already into the age of my second day of reasoning.

Okay, Nicholena, keep cool. I was calling myself Nicholena because when Richie said it, I felt secure. I said, "Come Mary, we will find another stable. Anna Muldowney heard me. She was the donkey's head. The ass did not fully understand me. Therefore, right in front of an entire audience, I had to improvise. I tried to turn the donkey around but the ass did not hear me. Right in front of the packed auditorium, the donkey split in half. The Blessed Mother went flying off the donkey. She was wearing yellow polka dot panties. The audience roared with laughter. Father Finnegan yelled, "Close the curtain, close the curtain." The audience clapped and roared with laughter. I thought Father Finnegan was going to congratulate me for trying to save the day; however, he did not see it that way. He said, "I want you to kneel in front of the Blessed Mother's statue and tell her you're sorry." I knelt in front of the Blessed Mother's statue, but I did not say I was sorry. I should not have been kneeling in front of the Blessed Mother's statue. I did not forget my lines. He rationalized that I should have stopped at that moment when the stable keeper told me that there was no room at the stable. We could have regrouped without making a mockery out of the Nativity pageant. I thought cut me a break. I did not reason all that out. I just reached the age of reason yesterday. My mother came to where I was kneeling and took me home. I think for the only time in her life, that she would have done combat with the good priest. He did not say a word when she took me home. Other people on the way home did. Mrs. Gradel said, "I thought that was the funniest thing I ever saw." Mrs. Banning said, "Joanie, you took the people's minds off of Pearl Harbor for a short time."

That was my job that day on Sunday, December 7, 1941, to take the people's mind off of the horrific news of the day, if only for a short time.

CHAPTER 18

The next day was the feast of the Immaculate Conception. December 8 was a Holy Day of Obligation. We were obligated to attend Holy Mass. There was no attending the night before the feast day. We needed to show up on the feast day itself. I looked at the statue of Mary and talked to her. I told her about Father Finnegan and his misinterpretation of my decision to turn the donkey around. I knew Mary would understand. I loved the Blessed Mother, and I knew everything was okay between her and me.

With that settled, I came home for breakfast. We always had off from school on Holy Days of obligation. The radio was on. My parents did not have the radio on all the time but it had been on since Sunday morning, December 7, 1941. On December 8, 1941, the holy day of obligation, the day after the bombing of Pearl Harbor, Roosevelt appeared before a joint session of Congress. Grimly, he described December 7, 1941 as "a date that will live in infamy." He then asked Congress to declare war on Japan. Three days later, Germany and Italy declared war on the United States.

World War II was already two years old when the United States joined the Allies. The forces of democracy faced dark days ahead. However, even most Americans who had defended isolationism now joined in the fight for freedom. Today World War II is like ancient history. I asked some high school students questions about World War II. Nobody knew the answers to the date that lives in infamy. In our neighborhood, the kids got busy. Over ten million men were drafted during World War II. My three cousins Jimmy, Richie and

Sammy Wootten were over there fighting for us. I will never forget the feelings I had about them. Wow! How could they summon up so much bravery? Then I remember Richie saying, "Nicholena, I will never, ever let anyone hurt you." He kept his promise. He went right over there after the tyrants of World War II.

The kids in our neighborhood sacrificed; little red wagons were appearing without the rubber around the wheels. Rationing went into effect. Sister Mary Augusta passed out our rationing books. My brother Bobby stopped adding Captain America and other comic books to his collection. He put them in the paper pile that was to go to the rag shop. We bought liberty stamps or war stamps from Sister Augusta. When the book was full, we could then exchange it for a war bond. Celebrities sold war bonds. USOs (United Service Organizations) sprang up around the country to give members of the military a place to go. They enjoyed donuts, coffee and dancing. The Jitterbug was the rage. I wanted to be in that generation so I could dance the Jitterbug.

For Easter, chocolate and coconut Easter eggs were replaced with Victory loaves. They had cornstarch in them and molasses. My friends said that they tasted like dung. I liked them. Besides, every little sacrifice would go towards getting my cousins and all Americans back home to safety. Tin cans were saved and salvaged from the dumps below Oregon Avenue. Since we had ration stamps for shoes, sometimes we went to Joe's shoe store on "2" Street. A large box of unmatched shoes stood on the sidewalk in front of his black tiled front wall. It stood beneath the large storefront window. We would spend hours sorting through that box trying to find a matching pair. We usually found a pair that matched. Most did not match. They were twenty five-cents a pair if we found a matching pair. I asked him, how much for one. He asked, "Why would anyone want just one shoe?" I replied, Paul Humphry fell off the chicken truck and broke his right leg. He said, "<A>. I never thought of that." I told him about my cousin Pat who needed to wear one regular shoe, as one leg was shorter than the other was. She needed a custom-made shoe on her right foot. I also told him about the old woman who lived in a shoe. He said, "<A> you are a smart kid." I suppose I could sell one from the unmatched shoes. I asked, "How much?" He pondered and said, "thirteen cents." I told him I thought the purchaser should have the benefit of the division. Since he could not charge twelve and one half cents for one shoe, I told him he would be held in higher esteem if he sold one for twelve cents. Besides, if people did not have a quarter they could buy one and sometimes doctor up the other shoe that the person already had. He said, "Good logic, kid, I'll do that." I said, "Okay Joe. Bye." He said, "Wait a minute" and he gave me a nickel." Cachinga!

Every ethnic and racial group in America contributed to the war effort. A higher proportion of Native Americans served in World War II than any other group. More than one out of three able bodied Indian man was in uniform. There was less prejudice and discrimination during World War II; however, it would be a long time before civil rights was put into effect. There were struggles and murders. It was a fight against tyranny, just as we were fighting in WW II. The only difference was that the enemy did not wear Swastikas; they wore sheets. When I was refreshing my memories of my life in the South Philly waterfront district, I went to a settlement house where I went when I was a child. I took piano lessons. I did arts and crafts. We did so many fun things there. I talked to the man at the desk. He helped to refresh my memories. They were all true. I went there sometimes with Mrs. Dunlap to play bingo. They had many social programs in place in the 1940s.

He mentioned The Southwark House playing a part in another era of history. He told me that part of the Underground Railroad was under the basement where I played games and played the piano. I told him that I never knew that. He told me he would show me where it still stands. I followed him to the basement that I remembered from childhood. That is where I also played bingo. I told him I played bingo there and took some piano lessons there. He replied, "I have more to show you." I proceeded to follow him to another door. He opened it. He told me that part of the Underground Railroad was there right in that little cellar next to the cellar where I had spent many hours when I was a child. Of course, it was a different time period. I was impressed and asked if I may take some pictures. He agreed.

I then thought I would research The Underground Railroad. I went to the library and got books on it. I called Professor Charles Blockson at Temple University. He has researched and written books on the Underground Railroad movement. He had no knowledge of any part of the Underground Railroad movement being at Southwark House. I thanked the good professor for getting on the phone with me. He is such a busy, important man. I went to the library and took out all the books I could carry on the Underground Railroad movement. Oh, I learned a lot about following the river gourd and peg leg Joe and how blacks passed for whites on their way to Canada. I had to stop the Underground Railroad investigation and put the focus back on the topic I was writing about in the first place.

I discovered that the past and present are linked. If Roosevelt did not set up all the programs in the 1930s and 1940s, we would not be entitled to all the social reforms he initiated. There is a river where the past, present and future flows peacefully together. It is spiritual of course. It behooves nobody to live in the past or the future. All we have is now; however, what we have done in the past affects the here and now. What we do now will affect the future. What we reap, we sew. In addition, to quote the philosopher George Santyana, "He who forgets the past is condemned to repeat it." We must pray constantly. As I was taught, more things are wrought by prayer than this world dreams of. I believe it.

Let's remember Pearl Harbor became the song that everyone was singing after December 7, 1941.

The children in our neighborhood continued to sacrifice for the war effort. By 1942, prisoner of war camps started springing up all around the country. There was a German prisoner of war camp at Mifflin and Swanson Streets in South Philly. Now enters the Chicken Pluckers Gang. They initially would march in front of the German prisoners of war and sing: Hang Hitler! Hang Hitler! They would then spit and sing, "Right in the fuehrer's face." Eventually they realized that since the German prisoners were already there in our neighborhood, they might be able to do business with them. Then a silent pact was made. The Chicken Pluckers Gang would give the prisoners of war Camel cigarettes. They in turn would throw a chicken over the barbed wire fence. The cigarettes could be bought by anyone if they had the penny. They were sold as two-fers. That is two for one cent. I went there one day. It was on my way to Weccacoe. I did not want them to throw a chicken over the fence to me or anything like that. I was seven; I looked through the fence. A young German prisoner of war was standing there. He looked about fourteen years of age. He looked as though he could have been a member of my family. He had blond hair and blue eyes. The sky blue prisoner of war uniform he wore made his blue eyes bluer. I was not reasoning things out. I was just encountering another human being. I put a Hershey bar between the links in the fence. He came over and took it. He said "Danke" and I knew what he meant. I continued on to Weccacoe. When I went to bed that night, I realized that nobody wanted their son to fight a war. I thought of his family. I wondered from time to time if he ever made it home to safety.

I wrote to my cousins, Jimmy, Richie and Sammy Wootten faithfully. I was hoping that they were encountering some people who treated them nice. WAR IS HELL! I prayed for peace.

I made my first Holy Communion in second grade. Sister Augusta made such a fuss over her little rosebuds. She knew we would all be getting a bath and putting on powder. She made it so special. She taught us how to perform the sacrament of reconciliation.

Holy communion picture L. Joan Morrisroe R. Emily Keegan-

Southwark house Front and Ellsworth Streets
Philadelphia, Pennsylvania-

CHAPTER 19

I made my first confession shortly before my first Holy Communion. It was scary, because in those days, we were told we would go straight to hell if we withheld a serious sin. After many rehearsals, it came time to go to my first confession. I said, "Bless me Father, for I have sinned." He said, "Yes, child go on." I actually was making up sins but I did not know that then. I told him that I sold my mother's bean soup, one time. He asked me if she owns a restaurant. I told him no. It was supposed to be our supper, but I sold it. He wanted more information. I thought oh, my is serious. I believe now I was amusing the priest. He said, "Go on child." I told him that I tore my brother's comic book in half. I then copped a plea and told him it was destined to go to Sid Waterside anyway. He asked who was Sid Waterside. I told him and then I started to confess Sid Waterside's sin of cheating. He told me to buy my brother another comic book. I told him that my brother did not buy it. Mikey Slop gave it to him. He asked me where did this Mikey Slop get it. I told him the entire Mikey Slop story about my father being pulled out of the speakeasy where he was drinking beer with Mikey Slop. That was a long time ago before I was born, when my mother mandated, "the drink or the family." I told him about the speakeasy man, saying my mother was worse than Slop's wife was. He listened. He said, "Okay, my dear; but where did this Mikey Slop get the comic book?" I told him that Mikey was a truck driver and delivered the comic books to the various stores. They were bound in wire. Usually the top book cover was already

169

torn; he would then give it to my brother Bobby. The priest told me to say three Hail Marys and to forget about replacing Captain America. I then told him, "I also got drunk." He said, "What?" I told him I had not reached the age of reason yet. I told him the story. I then froze. I did not think that his heart could withstand another of my sins. He started to give me absolution and I had not confessed talking in church, yet. I could not interrupt him, so I left with that big sin still on my mind. As I was leaving the confessional, he said, "Promise me you'll stop drinking." I told him I already had stopped drinking.

Holy Communion Sunday was a beautiful day in May. We needed to fast from midnight in order to receive Holy Communion. The hymns were magnificent. I was transformed into a higher dimension.

Gift of Finest Wheat:

You satisfy the hungry heart
With gift of finest wheat,
Come give to us, O saving Lord,
The bread of life to eat.

As when the shepherd calls his sheep,
They know and heed his voice;
So when you call your fam'ly, Lord,
We follow and rejoice.

ଔଔଔଔଔଔଔଔଔ

Father Walsh then held an elaborate Communion breakfast in the school hall. As I was about to cross Reed Street with Sister Augusta, a car almost hit me. She saved my butt. She pulled me back out of harm's way. She said, "You know Joan, you would have went straight to heaven." What she did not know was that I held back a sin of talking in church. I did not think she would have been able to save my soul that day.

That is how it was back then. I longed to go to the same school where "the publics" went because they just taught kids. They did not scare the daylights out of a kid. Sister Augusta would never do that; not knowingly, that is. That is how she was taught.

Rosie the Riveter became famous and a song was dedicated to women in the work force: Rosie the Riveter-lyric and music by Redd Evans and Jacob Loeb:

Sister Augusta distributed our rationing books. We needed stamps for shoes. The adults needed them for gas, for sugar, for food. We continued to salvage scrap iron, rags and papers. Rubber tires were not to be found on little red wagons. The children participated in the effort to win the War. We had Victory gardens. Even if a modest amount of soil was anywhere on a person's property, it was turned into a vegetable garden. If owners of junk yards refused to sell scrap metal to the government for about eighteen dollars a ton, the agents of the War Production Board could invade the junk yard. They often did.

When the school year ended at Sacred Heart, there was much pomp and circumstances. Awards were given for various achievements. There was a Mass said in Latin. We answered in Latin. We sang Latin hymns. The all girls' choir was formed in 1942. We continued to pray for our service members. During the war years 1941-1945 Sacred Heart lost twenty-eight of its former pupils to World War II. Among them was my cousin, Corporal Samuel Wootten. Aunt Mary had a banner in her front window. It had three blue stars adorning it. It was replaced with two blue stars and one gold star.

Besides Sammy, the casualties included:

John J. Chambers ☻
Robert Fitzgerald ☻
George Adams III ☻
John J. Jefferrs ☻
Frederick Bartelli ☻
Michael Piscitelli ☻
John J. McGuire ☻
James French ☻
William Branton ☻
George Bretschneider ☻
Joseph Reilly ☻
Anthony Capaldi ☻
Walter Byrne ☻
Anthony Dougherty ☻
Joseph F. Barnett ☻
Henry Galloway ☻
John Augustin ☻
Augustine Tascione ☻
Nicholas Campellone ☻
David Killian ☻
Joseph Sherker ☻
William J. Brennan ☻
Henry Ostrowski ☻
William McNasby ☻
Joseph M. Lacy ☻
George Thisselwood ☻
Philip Maniscalco ☻

CRCRCRCRCRCRCRCRCR
Mine Eyes Have Seen The Glory

Mine eyes have seen the glory of the coming
of the Lord; He is trampling out the vintage
where the grapes of wrath are stored;
He hath loosed the fateful lightning
of the terrible swift sword:
His truth is marching on.

Glory! Glory! Hallelujah!
Glory! Glory! Hallelujah!
His truth is marching on.

Julia W. Howe, 1819-1910, Music: trad. American melody, attr. to William
Steffe, ca. 1830-1911

Six hundred and seventy parishioners fought overseas.

The summer of 1942 was spent celebrating victories. Patriotism
prevailed throughout the country. When our military would win a
battle, such as Midway, we had a Victory parade. I remember my doll
baby being dressed like Hitler and hung. A shoe polish applicator
was taken off the bottle and used to serve as Hitler's mustache. Of
course, I did not volunteer Suzie for that role; my brother Bobby did.
I became hysterical when I discovered Suzie was left hanging on the
lamppost after the parade was over. The adults went on to party
and forgot Suzie. I was hyperventilating when I finally reached our
house. My father had my brother climb the lamppost and rescue
Suzie.

We spent a lot of time on Weccacoe. We caught beautiful
butterflies. There were mushrooms growing along the railroad
tracks; however, we never touched them. We knew about poisonous
mushrooms. We did not want to take a chance. The beetles were out.
They were considered good luck. We picked wildflowers.

September came in the blink of an eye. I passed second grade
with excellence. I would now be getting Sister Mary Emily. She was

a quiet, mild mannered nun. She taught us well. She did not get as involved with us as Sister Augusta had; however, that was her style. She was a good nun. I especially got upset with God in November of 1942. The five Sullivan brothers were killed. A Japanese submarine sank their ship. They were all on the same ship.

When we had air raids and had to get under our desks, Sister Mary Emily did not recite Little Boy Blue with us as Sister Augusta did. Sister Augusta also had us sing, "Don't sit under the Apple Tree." I did not realize it then, but Sister Augusta had a strategy so we could identify with people sitting under things, such as haystacks and trees.

It did not seem to bother me too much, as I was older now. Although most homes had to have black shades on their windows, Sacred Heart's dark green shades sufficed. I recalled my mother's story of decorating with white shades when she was decorating her tiny, peaceful house on Mountain Street. However, times have changed. We now needed black shades. Sister Mary Emily did have one particular eccentricity. She always told the student that was adjusting the shades to make sure they were all the same length. She told us that if they were not, it is possible it could be conceived as a signal to the enemy. Our windows faced west on Moyamensing Avenue and the war was over there in the South Pacific and in Europe. Sister Mary Emily probably had a premonition from God. She just did not interrupt it as well as the prophets in the bible.

By now, I had my own circle of friends. We lived within a two-block radius. Since lunchtime was so long, (one-and one-half hours) we could take our time walking back and forth at lunchtime. We crossed Moyamensing Avenue with the guidance of a "Safety." We bowed our heads and made the sign of the cross when we passed the Sacred Heart of Jesus Church. We passed Little Gerritt Street. We did not need a Safety to cross us on Little Gerritt Street because a car could not fit on that street. Stories were starting to evolve about the big blue creepy looking house on the west side of Moyamensing Avenue. It was two doors away from Rodgers Funeral Home. We would stop and look it over. It was a Seaman's Institute in 1943. It still stands today. It is a rooming house. The only change I can detect is that it has two doors instead of one. The glass doors do not have a mail slot in the center like the gigantic wooden door had in 1943. It reminded me of a mystery. We told everybody about the threatening looking blue house. We continued our sightseeing trip home for lunch. My mother made us the hot dittalinis, the one-half inch pasta about the width of a drinking straw that were covered with melted cheese and tomato sauce. My mother always had a tall glass of milk set out for us. We were then given a piece of fruit that was in season. In those days, all foods had to be in season. We could not eat oysters in months that had a certain letter in them (not that I would want to eat oysters). We did not have the convenience of modern technology then. Things were simpler. On February 1, 1943, Franklin Delano Roosevelt sent a letter of condolences to Mr. and Mrs. Sullivan of Waterloo, Iowa. He sent his deepest sympathy and prayers for their sacrifice of their five sons: Francis Henry, Joseph Eugene, Madison Abel, George Thomas and Albert Leo. When the movie came out, I went to see it. It reminded me so much of a family that could have been right in our neighborhood. Thank God, I did not find out how George died until I was an adult. He was so disoriented from wounds and burns that his fellow survivors could not stop him from leaving the lifeboat. He wanted to swim back to the then sunken ship and get his brothers. A shark got him. I think that was the only time in my life I was actually mad at God. I thought, "How could you." WAR IS HELL!

Some of the wording in the hymns changed at Sacred Heart. Mary help us, help we pray help your children night and day became:

Mary help them, help we pray,
Help our soldiers, night and day,
Keep them from all harm and sorrow,
Mary help them, help we pray.

Find the liar, became Find the German spy. Never did anyone bring up the movie about the Sullivans. It was too close to home.

During February 1943, the FBI raided the big blue house on Moyamensing Avenue. The German spies were able to go to the rooftop of the giant house and watch which ships were coming and going on the Delaware River. When we peeped in the next day, we could see blood all over the walls. There was a German flag, tattered and torn with bullets. A former FBI agent also told me that the turrets on the Del-Mar-Va (Delaware, Maryland and Virginia) shore was there in the event the Germans made it on the shores of the Atlantic Ocean. Oh, they were a lot closer than most Americans dreamed. At the end of the war, Eisenhower demanded that the subs show themselves. German subs popped up off the coast of Cape May Point, New Jersey.

We kids in our neighborhood continued to do everything we could for the war effort. We gave up items so our servicemen would come back home, safe and sound. Harry Ladderback was a handsome six feet teenager when he enlisted in the army. He lived with his father in one of Bill Rodger's courts. Bill Rodgers now owned much of the property on Front Street between Tasker and Morris streets.

We received the news that Harry was in the Veteran Administration hospital. We did not hear what injuries he had sustained. Harry was coming home for Memorial Day. Every house in the neighborhood had some sign of welcome for him. Some had welcome home signs in their windows in anticipation of Harry's homecoming. When Harry arrived home, the first place he headed for was the Mom and Pop store on the 1600 block of south Front Street. He invited all the children that were around to join him, which we did.

Harry said, "Watch me," then chug a lugged an entire quart of Frank's orange soda. We were so impressed. He then bought a bottle of soda for every one of us. We thought that Harry must have really been thinking about the home based Frank's soda when he was over there. It was his celebration. He was home safe. We were enjoying the treats. We waited avidly for him to tell us about his heroism. We also thought he would show us his wounds if they were not in too private a place. In the midst of the celebration, a plane flew over in the skies of our neighborhood. Harry held his ears and ran outside through the line of kids. He crouched behind the Walkers' marble steps. He whimpered repeatedly, Oh, oh, oh, oh! Then we knew.

We were happy to hear that at least he was in the Veterans hospital and had not paid the ultimate sacrifice. However, had he? Would he be like Dominic with a fate worse than death?

Dominic was a World War I veteran. He was gassed. He received a pension from the government. He was a little man with hunched over shoulders. He never bothered anyone until the next generation of children started to tease him. He would then go after them. I knew the price that Dominic had paid for us. He went from garbage can to garbage can and ate food from them.

შოშოშოშოშოშოშოშო

Blessed Feasts of Blessed Martyrs

Blessed feasts of blessed martyrs,
Holy women, holy men,
With our love and admiration,
Greet we your return again.
Worthy deeds they wrought, and wonders,
Worthy of the name they bore'
We, with joyful praise and singing,
Honor them forever more.

o beata beatorum, tr. by John M. Neale, 1818, alt. Music Oude en Nieuwe Borenlities, c 1710

German spy house on Moymensing Ave-

CHAPTER 20

When a plane flew over the skies of our neighborhood, Dominic would crouch and hide just as Harry Ladderback did when he was home from the Veterans Administration Hospital. WAR IS HELL!

In June of 1943, I was promoted to fourth grade. We had the usual pomp and circumstances at Sacred Heart Church. Times are different, now. The Masses are said in English. Everything is more casual. Women do not need to wear hats to church. Men no longer wear Stetson hats to tip when they go by the church. Attire is more casual. The pomp and circumstances as I knew it is gone.

My cousin Elaine came to visit us from Riverside, New Jersey in July of 1943. She was sitting on our front marble steps with a beau. They were smitten with each other, she and Joe. I was eight going on nine years of age. I was hanging around and they wanted to be alone. Elaine, who was seventeen, suggested I go pack my clothes and she will take me back to Riverside with her. I said "okay." I heard her say, "That will get rid of her for awhile." Ah! I do not think so. During the war, we needed to have sand bags under the windows in case of an enemy attack. I thought the likelihood of that happening was slim. My cousins were over there fighting for us. I thought nothing like that could ever happen in the United States. I was a child. We had air raid drills. I remember one time I was coming home from the Lyric theatre when everything went black. I felt the walls of the houses and found my way home. It seemed surreal to me. I just did not think anything like that could happen here in the United States of America.

Since we had the sand bags under the bedroom windows and I heard her remark that my packing will keep me away from them for a while, I seized the moment. I think the sand bags were at least ten pounds. I needed to open a bag and take some sand out with my little shovel that I used for the beach or the vacant lot. I put the excess sand in a washtub. I then waited for a plane to go over our house. I gingerly poured the sand out of the bedroom window and then dropped the empty bag down onto the pavement. I made sure it was on the other side of where they were sitting. "My God," exclaimed Elaine. That plane just dropped a bag of sand." The neighborhood was aroused. Thank God that we did not have the modern technology that we have today. I would not have wanted to get into trouble with the government. Elaine was screaming about the plane dropping the sand. The air raid wardens came around. Before the police could be called, my mother happened to go into the front bedroom. She saw that a bag of sand was missing. She saw that there was a tub full of sand sitting in the front bedroom. She went downstairs and outside where all the commotion was. Oh, boy! I know trouble when it hits me on the head. What could I do? How about telling the truth? Daddy pulled up in his City car. He sold his personal car because of the gas rationing and shortage of rubber. Marie, Bobby and I were lined up for questioning. Andy was too young. I told the truth. I then rationalized that his relatives tricked me in 1940 when I did not reach the age of reason, yet. I told him that I made up my mind I would not be had again. I then copped a plea, and said, "I won't do it again, I just got upset, because they were trying to make a sap out of me." My mother used that word a lot. I think it stands for silly ass person. Daddy was stumped as to what punishment he would dole out. He said, "You are not allowed to go to Riverside, young lady, go unpack." I did not say anything, but I thought, "Elaine wasn't going to take me anyway, she just wanted to get rid of me." I knew when to quit when I was ahead, so I just followed his direction to unpack. I did not say anything, but when I went to bed that night after praying for everybody that I knew, I had myself a good laugh. That will show them. Gotcha!

The next day my friend Spike and I went to Weccacoe. We made several stops on the way. That is how it was; everywhere we went we stopped to see other things. We stopped at Stoney's in order to see the new shock machines that he had mounted on the wall of his store on Front Street. A person could put a nickel in the machine and hold the two knobs. They would then get shocked. I declined. I did not want to spend my nickels on shocks. If I needed shock treatments, my father had good insurance with the City of Philadelphia. Spike declined also. She was very rich. Then rich people do not spend their money for such things. I suppose that is how they get rich in the first place.

We stopped to pick up Carol on Mifflin Street. She lived down the street from the German prisoner of war camp. We then stopped and looked at the prisoners of war. I never did see that young German soldier again; however, I always wondered about him. As we were walking to Weccacoe, we heard people talking. By the time we walked the four blocks to Weccacoe, we had overheard about ten different versions of the sand bag and the airplane and the air raid wardens. My name was never mentioned once.

When I reached Weccacoe, I was able to reflect. I could have reflected negatively and really berated myself. I did not do that. Weccacoe was so special. I was enabled to think things through as I was picking wildflowers that beautiful summer day. It did serve to raise the peoples' consciousness that it could happen here. It did serve to get people rallied up for the war effort. Maybe that was my job that day. Maybe that is what God wanted me to do. Sid Waterside's salvage yard was overflowing with articles from attics, cellars, back yards. Everyone took stock and made contributions. They even contributed articles that they still could use. They thought that the war effort was more important. I knew that the War Production Board could come and take things if they were more useful for the war effort. They did not need to do that in our neighborhood. We surrendered things willingly. Even Sid Waterside cooperated. If he cheated the government, he would go to jail. Sid was a cheat, but he was not dumb. The Chicken Plucker Gang had as much shrewdness as the government; however, when he tried to cheat them, it did not mean he would go to jail. Besides, they cheated him right back by saturating the bundles of papers that they gave Sid.

On the Fourth of July in 1943, Marie and I were on the seesaw. We had the usual celebrations. We had the party on the vacant lot that had been converted into a playground. Marie and I were on the seesaw. When my end went up into the air, I got scared. I grabbed onto the bar, which held the plank that served as the seesaw. I watched my wrist turn around while my hand stayed put. It was my left wrist. I never saw anything like that. Blood gushed out and my bone stuck out. Knighty, who was one of the few people in our neighborhood who still had a car, took me to the hospital. He owned the bar at Front and Morris Streets. He did not have the usual brand new type of car that successful people and number backers drove. It had a wooden panel over the front door of the car. It was not designed that way. He rushed me to Mount Sinai hospital. I was rushed to surgery immediately. Since I had been at a picnic, I ate many things that would not be advisable for a person who was going to be given anesthesia. I can remember how sick I was after the surgery. A cast could not be put on my arm because it was a compound fracture and they needed to treat the wound besides the fracture. They put a board on my arm. It was wrapped in gauze. I was instructed what activities in which I could not participate. I could get a bath but I could not get the arm wet. I went back to the hospital one time a week for six weeks. I knew how careful I had to be. That is why Aunt Mary was crippled. Her leg was stitched up without the bone being set. Maybe, my grandparents could not afford both. My father had good insurance with the City so they could send me to surgery and stitch me up after setting my bones. <A>.

Shortly after I broke my arm, my Aunt Nellie died. She was only forty-two years of age. She had a fall down the winding steps of her Trinity house. It was difficult to maneuver while carrying anything up and down the winding stairs. I was so sad. Aunt Nellie was beautiful and witty. She had long auburn hair. I use to put her reading glasses on and run around her table. She would pretend she was chasing me. She would say, "Where are you?" "Where are you?" I cannot see. They were only reading glasses.

We had the ceremonious wake at our house. Mr. Haley came and put the wreath on the door. It had lavender flowers. That was Aunt Nellie's favorite color. People went by and made the Sign of the Cross. A gentleman tipped his hat. I was given lots of nickels. I put them in the cigar box, but I did not say Cachinga. I was too sad at losing Aunt Nellie. By now, my cousin Joe Gilbert from Riverside had been drafted. He was home on leave before being shipped overseas. He came to our house often that week of the wake. He helped as much as he could.

Aunt Nellie's wake had an Italian flair to it. My Uncle Doc's family brought all types of Italian foods. They brought crabs in pasta sauce. They brought pastry much like Dominic and Angelo would bring at Christmas time. Aunt Mary was running the vacuum cleaner when the discussion of beer came about. She wanted to have beer. My mother said, "No!" Aunt Mary told her the next-door neighbors had beer when Gus died. My mother said, "They are German and can handle their beer. I don't want beer around the Irish side of the family." Aunt Mary and my mother continued the discussion. Finally, my mother started screaming, "No! No beer." Aunt Mary turned the vacuum cleaner up to maximum cleaning setting to shut out the noise. This is something my prim and proper mother should have done years ago. Then they would not have been silently locking horns. I do not remember if the beer came or not, that was not my concentration. I had stopped drinking at five years of age.

On the night of the viewing people were in and out all evening. There were no formal viewing times in a private home. Bobby and I were in the front bedroom directly over the chimney where our fireplace stood in the living room. Mr. Haley had a big purple curtain in front of the fireplace. The coffin then was place in front of the curtain. It is amazing how a little decorating can transform a place. It looked like a palace. Our home was pretty and cozy, but now the colors and decorations served to make it look like a royal palace.

I asked Bobby if he felt like having some ice cream. Of course, he would not pass up ice cream. He said, "Yes." I said, "Okay, I'll go to the closet and get your bag of marbles. We will shoot one across the floor so mommy and daddy will know we are still awake. They'll come up and see that we need ice cream." Bobby told me how smart I was. I told him that I was eighteen months older than he was. He will learn as he goes along.

I suggested that we stake out the happenings downstairs first. We peeped down the stairs. There were two colored women with burka like outfits. I did not know what color they were. Their skin was darker than our skin. They were lighter than our Italian relatives were. Their burka type clothing was beige. They wore short head coverings. They were lying prostrate on the living room floor and chanting. I told Bobby they must have really liked Aunt Nellie. I never saw anyone affected by a person's death like that. I now know it was their custom. It was their way of praying. To them it was just like our having the priest from Sacred Heart come in to say the rosary.

After that, we went back into the bedroom. I went to retrieve the marbles from the shelf on top of the closet in the front bedroom. The chimney was next to the closet. The chimney was directly above the coffin. The chimney had a cover that was wrought iron. The marbles went flying everywhere. Our eyes bugged out. The ironing board fell out of the closet. I knew I had to think fast as this could be serious trouble. I was more concerned about the possibility that it would be taken as disrespect to Aunt Nellie. We would never do that, ever. I hurried and put the ironing board in the back of the door that was the entrance to the front bedroom. Bobby closed the closet door. We then sat down on the floor and shot a marble back and forth. That is until we heard all the commotion. We opened the door. It seems the dropped marbles went down the chimney through the openings in the wrought iron cover. The chimney was behind the coffin. My mother and father led the parade. Following were the Irish, the Italians, the Jews, whites, blacks and the burka dressed women whose color I did not know. Everybody that was downstairs was spooked. Now we had the League of Nations in the front bedroom. We did not plan it that way. I did hear something about the best-made plans of mice and men often go astray. Eventually it all worked out. My mother said, "Oh, you're still awake?" I told Bobby to let me do the talking, as he was just a little too honest. I answered, "Yes, what was all that commotion?" The best defense is a good offense. So much was happening that the story never was pieced together. I told them that maybe some ice cream would enable us to sleep. It was now about ten p.m. My cousins' Aunt Trixie told my father she knew a place on Ninth Street near the Italian market that stayed open until midnight. They went there and bought us vanilla, chocolate and strawberry ice cream. There was a tan looking topping, which was caramel. There were jimmies and whipped cream. What a feast! We ate the treats and fell fast asleep. When we awoke in the morning the only other person in the house was Mrs. Parker who was tending to Bobby and me. My Aunt Alice had Marie and Andy stay over their house.

When everyone returned from the funeral, another feast was put on the table. I did not feel like eating. I was thinking of Aunt Nellie, I cried until I fell asleep. When I awoke all of the people were gone except our family. I ate some, but I was really, sad. Little did I know then that was only the beginning.

CHAPTER 21

By now, I had been watching movies at the Lyric theatre. I liked that generation of young women. They waited at home for their loved ones to return. They wrote romantic letters back and forth. The women sprayed perfume on the letters. I watched it all. I liked the songs. Oh, everything seemed so romantic. I remember the stanza from the song "As Time Goes By" music and lyric by Herman Hupfeld.

I watched the glamorous movie stars write letters to their loved ones who were over there fighting. I received an idea. I watched them carefully as they played the parts of ordinary young women in America who waited for their loved ones to return. They had beautiful writing paper. They sprayed perfume on the envelope. They kissed the back of the envelope so a lipstick kiss would show.

I decided when we went to the 5 & 10 store, I would buy writing paper and envelopes with my usual treat money. I selected a beautiful lavender color with envelopes to match. I started to write to my cousins. I then learned that they had to be microfilmed and censored. Names, places or anything that could aid and abet the enemy were blacked out. "Loose lips might sink ships."

Back home, the moral was kept up by having Victory parades in our neighborhood. V became the sign for victory. Winston Churchill made the sign famous. It became the allies' resolve sign that they were going to win the war.

The young women of that era looked so glamorous. There was leg make up to create the illusion of stockings. Eyebrow pencils drew the lines on the back of the legs. Nylon was unavailable. It was used to make parachutes. The Eisenhower jacket became very fashionable. Our country liked Eisenhower. The women showed it by wearing his favorite waist length jacket.

CHAPTER 22

I liked the Jitterbug. I saw them dancing it at The Stage Door Canteen. Movie stars melted in with our military men. A song was written by Irving Berlin entitled: I Left My Heart at The Stage Door Canteen.

Bob Hope brought their USO shows to the South Pacific. Bob Hope brought his show anywhere that he could. He never was home for Christmas. The movie stars volunteered to go also. I remember some, Ginger Rogers, The Andrew Sisters, Frances Langford, Kate Smith and hordes of others. They especially concentrated on visiting our wounded in various hospital wards. Glenn Miller lost his life on a flight going over to France for a concert. The plane was listed as missing, however; it has never been found. His music lives on. I always liked Moonlight Serenade and String of Pearls. I remember Jane Froman singing Back Home in Indiana. Indiana represented every hometown in America.

By now, the evening newspaper of Philadelphia started to list the causalities from the Philadelphia, New Jersey area. Their pictures were shown. There would be at least two full pages of casualties listed every day. I recognized someone from our parish from time to time. I prayed for them. Some I did not know personally, but knew the family names. I prayed harder for my cousins who were writing to me faithfully when possible.

The summer of 1943 was a tough time for me personally. I not only suffered the compound fracture of my left wrist at the Fourth of July picnic. Shortly after getting the board and bandages off my arm, I suffered a seizure. I was running a high fever. It was a hot summer early evening. My father came home from work and initially sat with me doctoring me up with cold compresses as Doctor Devlin had suggested. My father did that until I fell asleep. He then sat on the other side of the maroon, mohair couch and dozed off. My mother was out on the front step. People always sat on their front steps then. My mother came into the house. I woke up. I asked her if I might have a navel orange. She complied. I sat up and peeled the orange. My mother saw that all was secure and went back outside. She returned in about ten minutes. I suffered a seizure, a convulsion. My mother did not wake my father; she panicked. She ran outside and grabbed Ducky, a sailor who was home on leave. He lived on Fernon Street. He had a big long Lithuanian name that started with Duck. That is how he received the name Ducky. Ducky followed her into the house. He said, "We need to get her to the hospital." Daddy had his City car that was now painted red. He took me to Mount Sinai hospital. They kept me. Dr. Lipshutz came in and looked at me. I already had been assigned a room in the children's ward. No one was allowed behind the glass partition in the children's ward. I saw my parents looking through the glass partition. The doctor started to swab my throat. I asked him to stop, please. I did not have a sore throat at all. I did not even have a tickle. There was no knowledge about hypoglycemia then. Fever, sugar from the navel orange; that about did it. I know that now. I did not know it then. I did know that I did not have a sore throat. He would not listen to me and continued to probe and take a culture from the tissues of my throat. I asked him politely one more time. He ignored me. I then blurted out, "What's the matter with you, you son of a bitch? Can't you understand English?" The red headed nurse who had a remarkable resemblance to Rita Hayworth, the movie star, gasped. The curtain had been pulled around my bed. My parents went to get a bite to eat. The doctor told them he would be working on me for about fifteen minutes. Oh, boy! My mother and father were reassured that I would be okay. My mother than sent my father home to tend to the other kids. He said he would pick her up after visiting hours. My mother was summoned to the doctor's office. Before he told her what he diagnosed was wrong with me, he sternly said to

"The Queen." "Mrs. Morrisroe, In the future I think you should watch your language around your daughter." My mother asked what he meant. He told her right up front. There was no beating around the bush. He said, "She called me a son of a bitch." My mother was livid. It was not exactly because of what I called him. I think The Queen was livid enough to agree with me. She glared at the doctor and declared, "I'll have you know I have never said a curse word in my life. What makes you think she heard it from me, DOCTOR?" She went on to say that, her family arrived in America on schooners. He cleared his throat. He went on to say that the child heard it from someone. Never! My mother, the queen was now irrational. She never once stopped to think of all the lovely words that came out of our neighborhood. He is lucky I did not call him "shit legs." I use to hear some of the stevedores pick up their baby and say, "How's my little shit legs?" I heard many words that I could have used. However, that was the first one I recalled. Thank God! A son of a dog was not as bad as some that I could have recalled.

My mother never let that one go. She recited it until her dying day. "How dare he?" She took the heat. As my mother was leaving, Father Cavanaugh was entering the children's ward. I think they called him. He did not mention it. He talked to me nicely.

Father Cavanaugh was the best priest I have ever encountered. His demeanor was not threatening. He had red hair and blue eyes. They showed he had a good soul. He asked me how I felt. He told me that he would pray for me to get better. I could talk to him and I did. I told him the doctor was going after my throat. I told him I did not have a sore throat. I told him I never had a sore throat. I told him I was scared, as I did not know what that doctor had in mind. Maybe he thought I was a Nazi and was trying to get back at me. I just did not know. Father Cavanaugh assured me that the doctor knew I was not a Nazi. Nazi's did not attend Sacred Heart School. That relieved me for a while. Father Cavanaugh blessed me and left. I then thought. We did have an Adolph at Sacred Heart School. That was his cross to bear during the war years. He was the most gentle, kind person I ever knew. We simply called him "A." We knew when to hold, we knew when to fold 'em. The next morning I was taken to the operating room and my tonsils were taken out. I then started wondering if the doctor was a Nazi. I could not voice it.

When I started school in September of 1943, I was assigned the most beautiful nun. She was tall, slim and could have been a model for a movie star nun. She reminded me of Ingrid Bergman who starred in The Bells of Saint Marys with Bing Crosby. That was the extent of it. I knew it as soon as I entered the room where I was to spend fourth grade. The logistics were bad. She sat us in alphabetical order. I sat in a double desk with Walter Morrell. It was next to the last aisle near the windows. In 1943 and 1944 beanie caps were the fad. We wore them all the time. We pinned charms on them. Walt Morrell leaned over and knocked my beanie right off of my head. It landed on the floor besides my desk. I in turn gave his a good whack. His beanie flew off his head and landed an aisle away where Sister Mary Bernadine was writing on the blackboard. She picked it up. She did not even have the usual brownie pick it up. She picked it up and brought it right over to me. She stood there. She glared down at me. She said, "Hold out your hand, Miss Morrisroe." I copped a plea. I told her I could not be hit on the hand with a yardstick because I just had a cast removed. I went into the entire story of my compound fracture. She did not budge. She asked me what arm it was. I told her it was the left arm. She told me to hold out my right hand. Again, I tried to cop a plea. I told her how terribly sick I had been. I told her about my mother pulling a sailor into the house. I told her I was in Mount Sinai hospital for a full ten days. There was no mercy. She glared down at me and said, "So you are the one who disgraced Sacred Heart of Jesus parish by calling the doctor a vile name." A Vile name? I did not know where that came from. I called him a son of a bitch in English, plain English. It reminded me of a game called "Whisper down the Lane." By the time, the story reaches the original storyteller it is an entirely different story. Vile, I never did hear of a country called Vile.

I was trapped. The doors were on the other side of the room. Trapped, no escape. I think of a young girl by the name of Anne Frank who was trapped. Of course, it would not be until years later that her diary was found. She lived in a small space in the attic of a sympathizer's house. It had rats. She made the best of it. She also wrote. That writing will serve to remind humanity that the Jews were targeted. They were not the only ones targeted; however, they lost over six million people to the holocaust, the most. There was heroism all around. I think I would have taken that chance; that is just how I am. I could not turn my back on them or any of humanity who were being treated unjustly. It did not make any sense at all. Why? Because a maniac was in charge.

The kids in our neighborhood continued to sacrifice for the war. They gave up desires to have bikes, wagons or any other item that may serve our country better. Jake Rabinowitz put out his usual display of toys the day after Thanksgiving in 1943. He had a professional window decorator put shelves in the window of his hardware store on "2" Street. It looked like a fantasyland. There were Shirley Temple dolls, red wagons, toy rifles and a beautiful Schwinn bicycle. There was every toy imaginable including the metal clown bank that would open its mouth so a coin could be inserted.

I wrote a Christmas letter that I gave to Santa's helpers at the Thanksgiving Day parade. Gimbels Department Store sponsored the parade. The culmination of the parade was when Santa climbed up to the top floor of Gimbels from a fire engine ladder. My father drove the sled for Santa one year. After that, we would get letters in our mailbox requesting various items from Santa. One child, Billy Wootten thought my father was Santa Claus. Most of the children thought he just had an in with Santa.

I told Santa in my letter that I would like to have a Schwinn bicycle. I also went on to say I would understand if he couldn't deliver it because of the military's need for rubber and scrap iron and all the things that served to support our troops. I just wanted to voice my desire. I much rather have my cousins home safe. I wanted it all to go away. I wanted all our fighting men, most of whom were just boys, back home in the United States of America.

My father knew about my letter. He sat me down and told me what I just told you. He reiterated that rubber and all the materials that a bike was made of were scarce. I told him that I understood. I knew I would not be getting a bicycle that year for Christmas of 1943. One evening shortly before Christmas, I walked down into the cellar of our house. My father had what I thought was a bicycle. He told me to go upstairs, immediately. I thought I would not be getting a bicycle for Christmas that year. I remembered the conversation with my father about the war effort. I knew my father would never intentionally trick me. I thought he was making me a bicycle. I thought he had salvaged items that the War Production Board did not want. My father could put anything together. He was a genius. Since I got a glimpse of a bicycle, I knew I would be getting it for Christmas.

On Christmas morning of 1943, I came downstairs and saw the most beautiful light blue girls' bicycle. I could not wait for the Christmas morning ceremonies were over to ride it that afternoon. It was a cold, damp day. I was dressed in my new Christmas clothes and felt as snug as a bug in a rug. About one p.m. I took my bicycle out for the very first ride. I did not know how to ride a bicycle. I fell two times. I got grease on my beige cotton stockings. I did not mind. Some people on Fernon Street came out to see my new bike. Cass Rice gave me a giant chocolate candy shaped like Santa. It had red and silver foil wrapped around it. Wow! I had it all to myself. I must be dreaming. I then fell and scraped my knee. It bled. I did not think people bled in dreams. Mrs. and Mr. Dunlap came out to look at my bicycle. He always playfully called me "Mrs. Jiggs." They gave me a quarter. Wow! I then rode around the corner to show Aunt Mary. She asked, "Are you going to write to the boys and tell them?" I said, "Yes." I became very sad for a few seconds. I longed for them to be home unharmed. Home, hometown, all was part of the American lingo during World War II. Richie, Jimmy and Sammy Wootten had lost their mother shortly after the war started. Aunt Mary became a mother figure to them. She and their mother, my Aunt Mame were very close. Aunt Mary and Uncle Sam never had children of their own. The boys wrote her all the time. They sent silk covers for pillows from various countries. They were placed over the sofa pillows that adorned Aunt Mary's couch in the living room. If they needed anything special, she was right there for them. Aunt Mary gave me a dime. Wow! I now had enough money to go to the ice cream fountain at Linsky's drug store. I parked my bicycle outside; no lock, no chain or anything to assure it would not be stolen. I ordered a giant banana split. I thought heaven must feel like this day. I wished it could last forever. I finished my banana split and then headed for Sacred Heart convent. I asked for Sister Augusta. All of the nuns came out to admire my new bicycle. I told them my father had to make it for me from salvaged items that the War Production Board did not want. They looked at each other. Across the side of my new bicycle was the word Schwinn.

In late autumn of 1943, I wrote my cousin Jimmy and asked me to send me a Jap's ear. Although he was in France, I thought everybody was fighting everywhere. I told all my friends as I thought Jimmy would comply with any of my requests. The day after Christmas in 1943, I came out of the Lyric theatre. There were about seven kids waiting for me. I heard the screaming and yelling. They were trying to talk in unison. Finally, I realized what they were saying. They told me my Jap's ear had arrived. It came in a little box addressed to me. We all ran to my house. We ran and ran until we were out of breath. I tore the paper off the box. Everyone was waiting in anticipation. The opening of the box revealed the most beautiful miraculous medal I had ever seen. It was marquisate and pearl. It more than made up for it not being a Jap's ear.

When Aunt Mary read her fortune cookie on New Years Eve, it read, "Be strong, life is sweet and sour." She was puzzled as she was a great believer in signs from heaven.

The year 1944 premiered with hopes of victory. The Mummers did parodies of all the axis powers. It served to enable people to feel connected to each other. We were not alone. Hitler was killed so many times in parodies that he finally did commit suicide. He was not just a lunatic. He was a coward as well.

I survived fourth grade. I was promoted to fifth grade. I received a couple awards. One was for not missing a day of school for the entire year. Now, that was tough for me. I was in a room where the logistics were bad for me. I also received an award for congeniality. I was a happy kid. I liked most people, in our country, that is.

I did not take time to hate the mad dictators. I just prayed and prayed that God would work things out and they would get their just due. I concentrated on our boys. I prayed for all of them. Sacred Heart had twenty-eight casualties of war. The Philadelphia Evening newspaper listed them. They were not all killed in the same battle; however, the D-Day invasion took many lives from our parish as well as every part of the country.

I was now in fifth grade. I was assigned Sister Edmund Frances. She was a quiet, unassuming nun. I needed a reprieve from the brutality of the beautiful nun from the previous grade. I did not remember much about Sister Edmund Frances. My memories were refreshed when I went to Sacred Heart of Jesus rectory in 2006.

Sammy Wootten's birthday was July 26. He was going to be nineteen years of age. He requested a new watch, when Aunt Mary had asked what he wanted for his birthday that year. She complied. She sent him a watch. She sent it in June so he would be sure to get it before his birthday. Several weeks later, she received the watch back, which read "UNDELIVERABLE" on the package. She thought maybe he was transferred somewhere where they could not deliver it. She sat at her cherry wood secretary desk and wrote him a letter. As she was signing off the letter, her bell on the front door rang. She answered to observe a Western Union man standing there with a telegram:

WE REGRET TO INFORM YOU THAT YOUR NEPHEW
CORPORAL SAMUEL WOOTTEN IS MISSING IN
ACTION stop

Aunt Mary and the entire family were stunned. I ran to my bedroom and got down on my knees. "Please God, find Sammy." I was scared. He spent part of his last leave before being shipped over there, staying with me. I could not go to the movies with the family because I had a slight fever from swimmers' ear. That is what he wanted to do. We had so much fun together. I was so proud of him in his uniform. He was not tall like his brothers. He reminded me of Audie Murphy, the hero who went on to become a movie star. He was like a big brother to me.

I asked my friends if they wanted to take a walk to Weccacoe with me. They agreed, as they were very upset as well. We passed the German prisoner of war camp but did not even look at it. We kept walking to Weccacoe. We did not catch butterflies that hot summer afternoon. We just watched them fly into the heavens. We picked some wildflowers. When we came home, I brought a picture of Sammy outside. I asked my mother if we could light a candle and put the flowers from Weccacoe in a vase in front of his picture. She said, "Of course." I asked anyone who was around to pray for him. We held a candlelight service.

CHAPTER 23

About one week later as we were coming out of the candy store at Front and Mountain Streets, we observed a big black car turning onto Mountain Street. We followed it. It was going very slow. It stopped at Aunt Mary's house on Mountain Street. Two soldiers alighted from the car. They gave Aunt Mary the news. Sammy had been killed in Normandy, France. Oh, my God! We all froze in our tracks. My cousins, Eleanor Powers and Jean McGovern went to Nuny's workplace and broke the news to her. Her brother Sammy was killed in action.

Nothing made sense that day. I went to Weccacoe. I wanted to be alone. I wanted to scream. I wanted to cry. I wanted to wake up from this nightmare. I just looked at the flowers, the butterflies, the ladybugs and the occasional frog. I stayed for about one hour. I was not able to pray but I fingered my rosary beads. I walked home slowly. People did not talk to me on the way home from Weccacoe. It was too incomprehensible. Many of the people that I passed were related to us. Everyone kept their heads down to hide the tears. Several weeks later when the Philadelphia Evening newspaper listed the casualties, Sammy's picture was on the left hand side of the page. On the right hand side of the page was my other cousin, Joe Gilbert of Riverside, New Jersey. WAR IS HELL! There were two full pages of casualties from our area. Near Sammy's picture was that of Henry Ostrowski. His family lived on the next block down from us on Front Street. He was a twin.

We went to Sacred Heart of Jesus Church for a memorial type of service for Sammy. There was a coffin draped with an American flag. On top of the coffin sat a little box. I know one of the items in it was The Purple Heart. There was nothing left of him to be sent home. The soldiers came. Father Walsh had all the pomp and circumstances. The hymns were magnificent. Chills went up and down my spine when I heard, America.

☨

My country 'tis of thee,
Sweet land of liberty
Of thee I sing;
Land where my fathers died,
Land of the pilgrims' pride,
From every mountain side
Let Freedom ring!

Samuel F. Smith, 1808-1895, Music" Thesaurus Musicus, 1744

For years, we were under the impression that Sammy had been killed in the D-day invasion. With modern technology, we were able to determine that had not been the case. He had survived the invasion. He was standing around a truck on June 19, 1944 with three other soldiers. It was booby-trapped. It exploded. All that were left were the dog tags. Aunt Mary refused to believe it. She stayed on the denial step for a long, long time. She wanted to send my sixteen-year-old cousin Nuny over there to find him. When I think back, I can see I was in denial also. I looked at every newsreel at the Lyric theatre. Back then, it was all about the war. It showed the pictures of the soldiers. I looked for him for years.

Aunt Mary was the beneficiary of his insurance policy from the service. It enabled her to stop working. She had to go to work at age fifty after Uncle Sam died a few years earlier. She also always provided for Sammy's brothers and sisters. From time to time, someone would be living with her. Nuny lived with her until she got married.

Richie and Jimmy Wootten made it home, safely.

I learned how bittersweet life could be. I learned that I must continue trying, no matter what. My father was not in the service;

however, we had a new addition to the family in the baby boomer generation, in 1946. My sister Eileen was born on October 9, 1946.

I remember the post war excitement. There were cars galore on the assembly lines again. G. I.s could buy houses in suburbia such as Levittown in both Pennsylvania and New Jersey. Suburban communities were springing up all over the country.

In 1948, I graduated from Sacred Heart School. I was now looking forward to going to Hallahan High School. My trips to Weccacoe became more infrequent. I was now turning into a young lady.

In June of 1950, I had a need to go back to Weccacoe one more time. It was on that day that I realized what Weccacoe was.

On the Delaware River at Mifflin Street, two blocks from Weccacoe there were the remains of three wrecked ships. They were sitting there ever since I could remember. We called them the Three Sisters. The boys in our neighborhood swam off them, despite being warned that the mighty Delaware could be mighty dangerous. On that late sweltering summer afternoon, several boys decided that they would go swimming off the remnants of the wrecked ships. My brother, Bobby declined. He needed to serve the Philadelphia Evening Bulletin Newspaper. Word spread fast in our neighborhood. The unthinkable, every parents' nightmare, a boy had drowned in the Delaware River at the Three Sisters off of Mifflin Street, two blocks from Weccacoe. Suppers were put on hold that infamous day. Nobody had an appetite. The families were praying that the boy would be found. No one knew yet if it had been his or her son or someone else's son. They did not seem to be focusing on who it was. He was somebody's son. They all stood together, praying, crying, hugging each other and waiting. The waiting was what took me back to Weccacoe when daylight was slowly ebbing into dusk.

I had been breeding larvae into potential butterflies. I do not know why but I took the breeding apparatus with me. I had been watching closely to witness the metamorphic process.

My friends Marion Egger and Peggy Banning went with me. We carried empty mayonnaise jars in order to catch the fireflies. When we arrived on Weccacoe, it was brighter than any natural light that the brightest sun could produce. There were searchlights. The Philadelphia Police Harbor Patrol and the Coast Guard Patrol were conducting a search and recovery effort. There were no fireflies to snare. We picked some of the beautiful wildflowers with colors of lavender, yellow, site, green and pink. We picked the cattail in between the flowers. We filled the jars frantically with the wildflowers, as if we were trying to put a substance back into a jar that had been filled and so conducive to enhancing the taste of a tomato sandwich on white bread which I ate in the summertime.

Suddenly, the searchlights went off. Weccacoe seemed blacker than ever before. The fireflies came out. We did not bother to catch them. We let them alone, to fly free up into the atmosphere, providing the only light that was left in that small neighborhood that evening. I looked inside the tent where I was breeding the larvae for butterflies. The metamorphous was complete. Some had more than one color. The colors were, as I have never seen, as if painted by a great master painter. There was blue. There was yellow, there was lavender. Some had brown, white, red and yellow intermingled in the solid color. I caught a glimpse of one that was smaller than the others were. It had red wings on most of the center. There were lines running across the wings, as if it was symbolism of life's cycles. We picked up our mayonnaise jars filled with wildflowers and walked the two blocks to Delaware Avenue and Miffin Streets. We stood in front of the Three Sisters wrecked ships. We gently emptied our jars full of wildflowers into the Delaware River where the boy's body had been recovered. We felt sad as we headed home. "Goodbye friend, until we meet again."

I went back to Weccacoe in the summer of 2006. Modern technology has replaced two of the three blocks that consisted of Weccacoe. One block was still standing. It looked the same as it did in the 1940s. The industrial buildings on the left have long been abandoned. The names of the buildings are obscured. There were still train tracks that extended west on Snyder Avenue for a short distance to Weccacoe. I probably will never see any parts of Weccacoe as it was, again. The Philadelphia waterfront is being transformed into an elegant rejuvenation. The Indians are coming back to the waterfront about three miles from where it all began. They intend to open a casino called Foxwoods.

Weccacoe means a peaceful place. I learned about life on Weccacoe. I learned about death on Weccacoe. Moreover, I learned that there is something Greater than ourselves out there. I call it the Holy Spirit. The Lenape Native Americans call it the Great White Spirit. Other nationalities call it by other names. The beetle is sacred to the Egyptians. The silkworm larvae spins silk then turns into a moth. The most important thing that I have learned is to tap into the Divinity that is inside each one of us.

I hope the Pagan babies found Jesus, because now I understand about His sacrifice. I am assured of going to heaven, if I follow his path. The justification is through faith.

I believe other good people will get there also, if they have Love and lead a good life.

CHAPTER 24

The firefly is a nocturnal beetle that comes out at night. It lights up the darkness. Like most of nature they go through a metamorphic process. The main objective of the female is to lay eggs. The larvae hatch within a month. They surface in early Spring until late Spring. The larvae feed until fall, then they burrow underground for the winter. Some remain there for two or three years. They go through their grand metamorphosis, emerging as adults to light up for a short time in the summer.

CREDITS:

Gloria Dei (Old Swedes') Church Parish Profile Book-permission granted by the Reverend Joyce Singer.

Southwark House

Archdiocese of Philadelphia-permission granted for use of Gift of Finest Wheat.
1977. All rights reserved

I have researched in good faith to insure that I have not infringed on anyone's copyright. In the event that I have infringed on anyone's copyright, I shall rectify it upon notification.

The same applies if I have not given credit to anyone.

There were many people who helped me with my research, for that I am grateful.

ABOUT THE AUTHOR:

Joan Morrisroe Reynolds has created this work in order to get through the untimely loss of her beloved son, Franny Malloy. Widowed at an early age, Joan went on to rear her children on her own, until she wed Bob Reynolds in 1975. She would not take no for an answer and obtained a mortgage on a home in the Far Northeast section of Philadelphia in 1970. Joan is an independent thinker, as evidenced throughout her entire book. After rearing her children, she went to work in the Social Work Department of Rolling Hill Hospital. She worked as the Office Manager and the Social Work Assistant; she attended Community College of Philadelphia while working at Rolling Hill. She graduated in two curriculums with honors: Social Services/Mental Health and Addiction Studies, which included Criminal Justice. She was able to do three of her internships at The Philadelphia Police and Fire Employees Assistance Center. She did an internship at Rolling Hill Hospital where she met the needs of geriatric patients. Joan then went to work at Warminster General Hospital where she coordinated an outpatient program for people with addiction problems. She also initiated family programs. She then went to work at the Livengrin Foundation, a full range treatment center for people with addiction problems. She went on to become a Behavioral Management Specialist. When Joan relocated to Fort Myers, Florida in 1997, she was again able to work with geriatric patients at Lee Memorial Hospital. Joan has a photographic memory and recalls her colorful childhood with a poignant description of the tragedies. She describes the patriotism that prevailed during World

War II. Events that she remembers from the World War II era are described eloquently. She describes other events of her childhood with hilarity and warmth. She draws on the human spirit as her guide.

Printed in the United States
125220LV00001B/48/P